CAESAR'S SWORD (III): FLAME OF THE WEST

By David Pilling

Copyright David Pilling

Follow David at his blogs at:
www.pillingswritingcorner.blogspot.co.uk
www.davidpillingauthor.com
http://www.boltonandpilling.com

Or contact him direct at:
Davidpilling56@hotmail.com

1.

No father should have to bear the loss of his son. Of all the cruelties and hardships God saw fit to heap upon my head, this was the worst.

Abbot Gildas, who knows something of my history, sometimes asks to join me in praying for the soul of Arthur. He does not know I pray for my son's wellbeing, not his soul.

I last set eyes on him almost twenty years ago, near the banks of the Po in northern Italy. If I shut my eyes, I can picture him clearly: a tall, proud, soldierly figure, with his mother's wiry frame and the flaming red hair of his royal British ancestors. He rode as well as any Scythian or Hunnish horse-archer, and Caledfwlch gleamed in his hand.

"Go!" I screamed, pointing my spear west, towards the distant border of Liguria, "go now, or bear a father's curse!"

Arthur might have disobeyed, for he was ever a strong-willed brute, but he carried a sacred charge. Caesar's sword, wielded by his famous ancestor (and namesake) at Mount Badon, could not fall into the hands of our enemies. I had made him swear an oath to that effect, and taught him to keep his oaths.

Our eyes met for the last time. His were green, so much like his mother's, and blazing with fury. It was against his proud nature to turn and run, but there was no help for it.

The thunder of hoofs sounded behind us. I twisted my neck and saw the dark shapes of horsemen thundering across the plain to the south. A dozen at least, Frankish lancers in gleaming mail and white cloaks.

They had been pursuing us for days, remorseless as hounds after a couple of fleeing deer. I tried every trick I knew to evade them, but the Frankish captain was no fool, and saw through all my deceptions.

I glanced back at Arthur. To my relief, he had obeyed my last instruction, and was riding away to the west at the gallop. We had fled with remounts, and ridden the first pair of horses to exhaustion, but his fresh mount would carry him over the border to safety.

He urged his horse up to the crest of a little ridge, and there halted and wheeled her about. For a moment his superb cavalry figure was silhouetted against a backdrop of rolling hills and the light of the rising sun, Caledfwlch raised high in salute. The length of the blade rippled with silvery light, as it had done in the caves on the shore of Amorica, so many years ago.

"Virtus et fortitudo!" I heard him shout: 'Courage and strength', the old battle-cry of the legions. My eyes misted as I recalled the

first time Arthur heard it, chanted by a phalanx of Isaurian spearmen marching on parade along the Mese in Constantinople.

Then he was gone, vanished behind the ridge, and the light of Caledfwlch snuffed out.

I dragged my horse around to face the Franks. They were coming on at the charge, triumphant war-shouts tearing through the still air. It was Caledfwlch they wanted, not me, but I would die rather than let them slay my son and deliver Caesar's sword into the hands of a barbarian king.

Blinking away tears, I urged my horse straight at the Franks, aiming for their captain. He was a typically burly officer, his auburn hair twisted into pigtails, face partially hidden behind the nose-guard and hinged cheek-pieces of an elaborate golden helm.

"Belisarius!" I shouted as I surged in for the kill, the name of my old chief rising in my throat. I had not shouted his name in many years, and would never see or serve under him again. Despite everything, all the bitterness and disappointment he had caused me, I still honoured the man.

The Franks spread out to encircle me. I ignored them and cast my spear at their leader. It was a good throw, and pierced his right shoulder, just above where a silver brooch held his cloak in place. The impact made him jerk in the saddle, and his horse came to grief, her legs tangling and folding up under her.

His men screeched in rage and closed in around me. I dragged back on my reins with one hand and reached for my spatha – a poor substitute for Caledfwlch – with the other.

A spear clanged against the shield strapped to my left arm. I bit back a spurt of pain, tore the blade free and turned to face the nearest Frank as he came plunging at me, axe raised high.

At fifty-one, my reflexes had lost their edge. I tried to lean sharply to my left to avoid the blow, but was too slow. The edge of his axe slammed into my breast. It split the mail, drove the breath from my body, and hurled me backwards out of the saddle.

Red blotches flashed before my eyes. The world spun crazily. My horse bucked and shrieked in panic. I landed with a jarring thump on my back.

I tried to rise, but a dark shadow fell over me, and flailing hoofs crunched into my ribs, my pelvis, my spine. One of the Franks had ridden his horse straight over me.

Pain, and numbing despair. I lay curled like a worm on the end of a hook, unable to move, scarcely able to breathe. Waiting for the blow that would finish me, and usher my shade into the next world.

It didn't come.

2.

I am ahead of my tale, and must go back some thirteen years, to the coast of Naples. There, along with Procopius and a few other companions, I saw the Roman fleet anchored in the glittering blue waters of the bay.

We had crept out of Rome, on the orders of Belisarius, to make our way through the Gothic siege lines and hence to Campania, to try and raise reinforcements from our scattered garrisons.

Procopius let out a cry of joy when he sighted the fleet. The troops from Constantinople were so long-delayed we had despaired of them ever arriving, and he was of the opinion that the Emperor Justinian had abandoned his army in Italy to its fate. Procopius always held a low opinion of Justinian, and those unfortunate enough to read his *Secret History* (as I have) will know how his dislike of the emperor eventually congealed into madness.

He had to swallow his bile on this occasion, and clawed at my arm in excitement as he watched the soldiers disembarking in the harbour. They were Isaurians, tough infantry from the rugged hill country near the borders of Cilicia.

"Look to the south," he cried, stabbing his finger at a point further down the coast, beyond the city. I strained my eyes to see, and thought I made out a thin column of dust. Then I caught the flash of sunlight on spearheads.

"More reinforcements?" I said. He nodded vigorously, his oversized head wobbling on the end of its skinny neck.

"Must be," he replied, lifting himself awkwardly into the saddle, "let us go down and meet them."

I fetched my horse from where I had tethered her, and together – there were eight of us in all, including six Hunnish warriors and a native Roman who had guided us through the Gothic lines – we rode down the coast road, skirting the white walls of Naples and heading south-east, towards the advancing trail of dust.

The banners of Roman cavalry soon became visible. They turned out to be a mixture of Huns and Scythians and Heruls, two thousand men in all. Having made landfall at Otranto on the southern Italian coast, they had force-marched across Campania to meet the rest of the Roman reinforcements at Naples.

We learned as much from their commander, a nobleman named John the Sanguinary. You will gather from his name what kind of man he was. I had known many hard, bloodthirsty officers in the Roman army, such as Bessas and John Troglita and Constantine, but John the Sanguinary beat them all.

The son of Vitalian, a treacherous general who had rebelled against the Emperor Anastasius and was finally murdered by Justinian, he lived under the shadow of his father's accursed memory. Constantly under suspicion, constantly aware of Justinian's displeasure, he had somehow survived to adulthood and looked to forge a career in the army.

If I had known how much trouble this man would cause me, and the Roman cause in general, I might have thrust Caledfwlch into his heart. As it was, I respectfully saluted the tall, leathery-skinned nobleman, and listened while he spoke with Procopius.

Belisarius' secretary was not the sort to defer to anyone, but even he seemed overawed by John's languid, aristocratic air, and (most unusually for him) made an effort to listen instead of dominating the conversation.

"Ye-es," John drawled after Procopius had provided a hasty explanation of how we had escaped from Rome, "so General Belisarius is still shut up inside the city, is he? I feared as much. The general is a decent strategist, but rather too cautious."

I was eating while he spoke, and almost choked on a bit of dried meat. Belisarius had risked his own life many times during the siege of Rome, and performed wonders in defending the city against obscene odds. This arrogant, perfumed young noble, in his rustling silks and polished lamellar armour, knew nothing of the hardships of war.

No-one heeded my spluttering. "I have studied the approaches to Rome," said John, shading his eyes to study the fleet bobbing at anchor in bay, "and I believe the garrison still retains control of Ostia, am I correct?"

Ostia was the main harbour with access to Rome, about twenty miles northeast of the city.

"Yes," replied Procopius, "but the Goths have seized the Portus Claudii. Thus we cannot get supplies into Rome via the sea."

John gave a limp little flick of his gloved hand. "Then the supply wagons will travel up the Appian Way," he said, "escorted by our cavalry. If they are attacked, the men can dismount and the wagons form into squares. A mobile fortress, yes?"

It was an original idea, and I started to wonder if John was something of a soldier after all. Our last detachment of reinforcements had reached Rome via Ostia, and he had the same notion.

We did not advance north immediately, but marched to Naples. I had no sooner found a billet than Procopius insisted I ride out with him, to look for more reinforcements.

Knowing my duty, though resenting it, I consented to be dragged all over Campania. The secretary was seized with one of his periodic bouts of furious energy, and in the space of two or three days managed to raise some three hundred men from various occupied towns and villages.

"Not a bad tally," he said as we cantered back towards Naples, exhausted from our labours, "we might have levied more, but it is dangerous to strip the countryside of troops. I don't trust the Italians. They need the presence of armed men to remind them of their loyalty to Rome."

"But they *are* Romans," I protested, "this is the heartland of the old Western Empire. Surely they regard our arrival as a deliverance?"

This was a point I had never fully grasped, and Procopius smiled thinly as he explained it to me.

"The Romans have done very well under the rule of the Gothic kings," he said, "far better than under the latter-day Caesars. Between you and me, Coel, the later Western Emperors were a pack of idiots. They threw away their empire with both hands. Rome, and Italy, have prospered since Alaric deposed the last Emperor and sent his regalia to Constantinople."

I glanced nervously at the line of horsemen behind us. At least a quarter of them were native troops, volunteers who had flocked to our banner.

"It is a hard thing, to submit to foreign conquest," I said, "even if the rule of the conquerors is beneficial."

I was thinking of Britain, the homeland I had not seen since childhood, and wondering who held dominion over her now.

After my grandsire's death, the land had collapsed into a patchwork of petty feuding kings and chieftains, like so many cockerels fighting over a dungheap. Perhaps another strong man had emerged from the chaos, to seize power for a time. Or perhaps the invading Saxons and their foul kin had overwhelmed the fragmented British kingdoms and made the land their own. Whatever the state of affairs, I had little doubt the mass of the people lived in abject misery, taxed and herded into battle by their native rulers, slaughtered and enslaved by the invaders.

Sometimes I entertained impossible dreams of returning to Britain at the head of an army and rescuing my country. Restoring good government and order, expelling the barbarians, and uniting the land under a High King. I even pictured myself seated on the throne, robed in purple and cloth of gold like Justinian, Caledfwlch gleaming at my hip, and all the proud lords of Britain kneeling before me.

Fond dreams, for an ageing ex-charioteer and thoroughly mediocre junior officer in the

Roman army. I was unlikely to see Britain again, or live much longer. Somehow, through various twists of fate, I had contrived to offend powerful and dangerous people, including the Empress Theodora, her friend Antonina, and the scheming eunuch Narses. It was only thanks to the protection of Belisarius, who smuggled me out of Constantinople before the net could close, that I still breathed.

Even in Italy, far from the imperial court, my enemies struck at me. Antonina, as was her habit, had accompanied her husband Belisarius on the campaign, and brought along her vile son Photius. Photius had tried to kill me at least once, during the Battle of Membresa. I survived that, and another assassination attempt outside Naples, and lived in fear and expectation of more.

"I must leave," I said suddenly, blurting out my thoughts, "I must quit the empire. It is my only chance of survival."

Procopius nodded slowly. "I am inclined to agree with you. I have never known a man with a such a talent for making enemies. I think your escape can be arranged, but not now. After this campaign is over, perhaps. Belisarius will not let you go just yet. He needs you."

It seemed absurd, the idea that Belisarius was so reliant on one lowly officer, but I had the virtue of being loyal. The common soldiers loved their general, who had led them to one victory after another, but his captains were a treacherous, backstabbing crew, jealous of his success and always looking to criticise his decisions.

"He may yet promote you to centenar," said Procopius with a dry chuckle, "or even higher, depending how desperate he gets."

Soon the walls of Naples became visible, a shimmering white line on the horizon to the west. Procopius was distracted by the glint of spears to the north.

"Gothic scouts, possibly," he muttered, "let's get a closer look at them."

We rode north until more horsemen came in view. Two columns arranged in double file, advancing at the trot in the direction of Naples.

I did a swift head-count. "Two hundred," I said, "they fly Roman banners. Someone else has been at work, stripping the local garrisons of men."

Procopius was piqued, for he regarded the task of collecting reinforcements as his alone. He thought John the Sanguinary was responsible, and cursed the young nobleman for the upstart son of a traitor all the way back to Naples.

We arrived to find the city in ferment, and one name rippling through the crowded streets:

Antonina!

The mere sound of it filled me with dismay. Belisarius had smuggled Antonina out of Rome, away from danger, and sent her south with a strong guard to await the outcome of the war in the peaceful tranquillity of Naples.

He little knew his wife. Antonina had taken up residence in the governor's palace, from where she immediately despatched agents to gather men from the surrounding province. To do her credit, she had no intention of wallowing in comfort while her husband fought to defend Rome, and did her utmost to send him military aid.

I was reluctant to let Antonina know my presence in Naples, but misjudged my own importance: she was already embroiled in fresh plots and intrigues, and betraying her husband on a nightly basis with one Theodosius, a staggeringly handsome young man and Belisarius' godson. I was no longer of relevance to her, though continued to live in fear of receiving an assassin's blade in my back one dark night.

When over five hundred men had been gathered, it was agreed that our cavalry should advance north towards Rome along the Appian Way, escorting the train of wagons, loaded with corn and wine, for the relief of the city.

Meanwhile our fleet, carrying three thousand Isaurian infantry, would sail for the port of Ostia. This was the plan devised by

John the Sanguinary, and none cared to contradict it.

"If all goes to pot," Procopius remarked sourly, "then at least we shall witness a swift end to the career of a most unpleasant young man."

Procopius was vindictive, and judged people on instinct. I could never fathom, for instance, why he took such a liking to me.

I shared some of his dislike of John, who struck me as arrogant, but he was the most senior officer present in Naples. His pretty ways and noble birth appealed to Antonina, who had no hesitation in naming him our commander.

I joined the cavalry, placing myself among the Heruls, and our little expeditionary force set out north.

To Rome.

3.

We followed the Appian Way, the ancient paved highway linking Rome to southeast Italy. I fully expected us to be attacked, and to have to fight our way to Rome over mountains of Gothic corpses, but our progress was unhindered.

"Vitiges is looking north," Procopius said confidently, "all his attention is fixed on Rome. He pays no heed to what is happening behind him. Fool! Belisarius is lucky in his enemies. Not one of the barbarian kings he has faced is his equal in war."

This was true, though Vitiges, King of the Goths, enjoyed a reputation as an able and ferocious soldier. I had never even seen him, though he was said to be a typical chieftain of his race, tall and auburn-haired and dripping with gold ornaments.

John the Sanguinary was less of a toy soldier than he appeared. He was careful to despatch scouts, to look for any sign of the Goths. They returned at a hard gallop when we were some five miles south of Rome.

"General Belisarius has sallied out from the Pincian Gate," one reported breathlessly, "almost his entire garrison is engaged with the Gothic host, in pitched battle on the plain before the city."

John's carefully plucked eyebrows shot up. "Not as cautious as you thought, eh?" I remarked, and returned his frown with a grin. In days of old I might have been flogged for insolence to a superior officer, but the legendary discipline of the Roman army was much decayed.

"It is a distraction," said Procopius, "Belisarius must have learned of our arrival, and has engaged the Goths to give us time to reach Ostia and meet up with the fleet. When he learns we have safely passed through the enemy lines, he will withdraw back inside the city."

John hesitated. The city lay to the north-east, and we were following the section of highway that led straight to the port of Ostia. Just visible to the north was the section of ruined aqueduct that Vitiges had partially repaired and turned into a fortress, guarding the approach to Rome.

"You," said John, stabbing a finger at me, "remind me of your name."

"Coel ap Amhar ap Arthur," I replied promptly.

"Ah, yes. The general's tame Briton. I have heard something of you. Brave and loyal, they say. Let us test those qualities. I want you to take five hundred men – the ones we levied in Campania will do – and ride north-east to assist Belisarius. The rest of our force will continue north and press on towards Ostia."

I stared at him, regretting my insolence of a moment earlier. "But, sir," I protested, "I am a mere infantry officer, and have never commanded more than ten men in the field."

He smiled lazily at me. "Then here is an unrivalled opportunity to prove your worth. You ride rather well for an infantryman. Let us see how you lead."

John was the commander, and there was no gainsaying his orders. I turned away, trying to ignore the jealous stares of the more senior captains who should have been sent in my stead.

Procopius touched my shoulder. "He thinks you will fail," he whispered, "but I have every confidence in your ability. Do well, and you may receive your promotion sooner than we thought."

My orders were to lead my new command north, straight through the heart of the Gothic camp, and do as much damage to the enemy as possible before withdrawing. I was fairly certain John didn't care about our fate – I was a mere Briton, a barbarian from the distant north, and my men were the scrapings of local garrisons – but wanted to ensure he got his two thousand cavalry to Ostia.

Feeling giddy, I put myself at the head of the levies and glanced up at their banner, flapping limply in the slight wind. It displayed the double-headed Roman eagle, worked in golden thread against a red field.

I had followed the eagle in a series of bloody campaigns, from North Africa to Sicily to Italy. For much of that time I had fought as a common soldier, free of the burden of rank and responsibility. My one stint as an officer, in charge of a handful of Heruls and Isaurians, had been mercifully brief. Arthur's blood ran in my veins, but not his natural talent for leadership.

Now John the Sanguinary had put me in charge of five hundred cavalry. My guts rumbled in panic as I trotted to the head of my new command. Swallowing, I raised my arm and nodded at the trumpeter to give the signal to advance.

I led them on at the canter, skirting the ruins of the aqueduct and aiming for some open, flat ground with a large timber stockade to the north-west. If the Goths should suddenly spring on us, at least we would have room to manoeuvre.

Tattered Gothic banners displaying their crude symbols of the horse and the bull flapped from the walls of the stockade, and the upper levels of the aqueduct-fortress.

I glimpsed a few helmeted heads, and expected the timber gates of the stockade to yawn open at any moment, disgorging thousands of screaming Gothic cavalry. They are fine horsemen, though they have no mounted bowmen as good as our Huns and Heruls, and enjoyed a massive advantage in numbers. Over a hundred and fifty thousand Goths were encamped around the walls of Rome, an entire nation in arms.

Nothing happened. The sentries ducked out of sight, and we thundered on past endless rows of empty tents and doused cooking fires.

It was unnerving. The whole of that vast encampment, spread out on the fields south of Rome, was emptied of troops. It was not deserted: we rode past tents full of sick and wounded men, and somewhere a war-horn sounded the alarm, but there weren't enough soldiers left to oppose us. We might have plundered the baggage wagons and set the rest of the camp on fire, but I was no freebooter, and stuck to my orders.

The sound of a gathering storm lured us north, towards the walls of Rome. As we drew closer, the sounds became more distinct; the rumble of hoofs, the shrieks of terrified horses and dying men, the scrape and clash of weapons - war-cries, screams, conflicting orders, war-horns sounding advance and retreat, the zip of arrows and barrage of drums. All the noise and chaos and terror of battle. It was a familiar, heady, intoxicating din, both terrifying and appealing, quickening a man's blood at the same time as driving him almost mad with fear.

I halted on a little rise overlooking the battlefield, drinking in the sight and sound of slaughter.

Thus far in the Italian campaign, Belisarius had suffered only one defeat in battle against the Goths, and this was down to the cowardice and indiscipline of the Roman citizens who insisted on fighting alongside our men. He had learned his lesson, and I compare the battle I witnessed before the walls of Rome that day as akin to a skilled boxer holding off a heavier, clumsier opponent.

Our horse-archers swarmed forward, isolating bands of Gothic footmen and riding around them in circles. Stranded, the Goths could do nothing but duck behind their large wooden shields as arrows rained down on their heads.

The slow, heavily armoured Gothic cavalry lumbered forward, but our men swiftly retreated in good order, behind the safety of their own footmen. These were drawn up in six disciplined phalanxes in front of the Pincian Gate.

Despite his overwhelming advantage in numbers, Vitiges' only chance of victory was to break the iron wall of Roman infantry. He threw his horsemen against the lines of shields time and again, like waves lashing at a rocky shore. Time and again the Goths were repulsed, leaving the broken bodies of men and horses strewn about the bloody, churned-up ground. Any gaps in the Roman infantry squares were quickly filled, plugged with fresh bodies from the reserves Belisarius had drawn up behind the front lines.

I could see the general's banner, fluttering above the heads of the infantry. His golden-armoured figure would be at the head of his bucelarii, elite Roman cavalry, waiting for the Goths to tire so he could lead them forward in a shattering, all-out charge. It was the same tactic he had used against the Sassanids at Dara, and the Vandals at Tricamarum, and on both occasions proved devastatingly successful.

It was midmorning, and the fighting had been going on some time. I thought Belisarius had advanced dangerously far outside the gates, beyond the defensive cover of the ditch. The Goths were concentrating their attacks on the exposed flanks of his infantry. If these were smashed the entire Roman line might be rolled up and destroyed.

Directly in front of my position, not thirty feet away, were the rear lines of the Gothic reserves. They were mostly infantry, armed with long spears and heavy shields, and had their backs to us.

I had to act before they noticed our presence. For a terrifying moment I was seized with indecision, the curse of men promoted beyond their station and ability. The blood ran cold in my veins. My fingers froze on the hilt of Caledfwlch, and the order to charge dried up in my throat.

Shaking with terror, I had enough presence of mind left to nod meaningfully at the trumpeter. He raised the curved bugle to his lips and blew a long, sharp blast, causing my horse to rear and toss her head in panic. I fumbled with her reins, my fingers slipping, and she bolted, straight towards the Gothic lines.

"Roma Victor!" I croaked. The strangled cry was taken up by my men, and then they were surging after me, baying like hounds racing in for the kill.

We were among the Goths before they knew what had hit them. I managed to regain control of my horse, and steered her with my knees, Herul-style, stabbing right and left with Caledfwlch.

My panic ebbed away. The Gothic spearmen scattered, their ordered ranks dissolving into a mob of confused and frightened men, taken unawares as they watched the battle unfold before the gates of Rome. They outnumbered my levies at least three to one, but we had the advantage of surprise.

I did my best to make it count, urging my horse deeper into their squadrons, bellowing like a mad bull. Caledfwlch was slippery to the hilt with barbarian blood, and my men did terrible execution, fanning out to strike down the fugitives with spears and spathas.

We carved a lane right through the centre of the Gothic army, until I found myself in the heart of the storm, surrounded by fighting men, on foot and horseback, stabbing and hacking at each other. Great clouds of dust rolled and billowed across the field, tinted by red mist. Bodies lay everywhere, twitching and bleeding in their death-throes. The ground was littered with broken weapons, fallen standards and bits of abandoned gear.

A division of Gothic cavalry were entangled with some of our infantry and a unit of horse-archers. My levies had crashed into the heaving, surging combat, and now all was confusion. Officers rode about like lost sheep, losing sight of their commands as Roman and Gothic banners dipped and mingled in the throng, a meaningless riot of colour.

I was fighting for my life, and had little idea of the general progress of the battle, but was later able to piece events together.

Belisarius had deliberately advanced too far beyond the Pincian Gate, and exposed his flanks to a Gothic counter-attack. Vitiges seemed to have forgotten who he was fighting, and blundered straight into the trap. At about the time my levies were making short work of the Gothic spearmen, Belisarius had sounded the retreat, and his entire army started to withdraw. Smelling blood, the Goths pursued with wild abandon, thinking they had the Romans at their mercy.

I knew little of what was happening, having lost touch with most of my command in the general chaos. The trumpeter and standard bearer had stuck close to my side, and I looked around for some high ground, where I might try to rally my scattered men.

A blast of trumpets and bucinae rose above the hellish, ear-splitting noise of battle. I glanced north, and saw the Roman banners moving away, back towards the grey walls of Rome. The eagle was retreating.

The Goths uttered a great shout of triumph, and the sea of bodies around me gave a violent lurch, as though a powerful current had run through it. I found myself carried along, helpless against the tide, crouched low over my horse's neck as enemy warriors stampeded past me, chanting their war-songs.

To raise my head in that heaving mass meant death. Somehow my horse kept her footing, and not one Goth stopped to turf me out of the saddle. They had a greater quarry to chase.

When the din had died down a little, I risked looked up, and found myself alone. The plain around me was deserted, save for a few scattered corpses and the occasional riderless horse, peacefully cropping at the trampled grass.

I gently turned my own horse about, and looked upon the destruction of the Gothic army.

The Romans had fled with all speed to the Pincian Gate, hotly pursued by the enemy. To the west, close to the banks of the Tiber, lay the Flaminian Gate, which Belisarius had ordered blocked up with rubble. I remembered doing my part to seal the gate, sweating in the Italian sun as I heaved lumps of stone onto the pile under the arch.

Unknown to me, and certainly to the Goths, Belisarius had ordered the stones removed during the night before the battle. As the Gothic cavalry rushed towards the walls, hoping to cut down our fleeing soldiers and force entrance into Rome, a single trumpet-blast rang out on the parapet.

The Flaminian Gate rumbled open and the bucelarii charged out, a thousand lancers in shining lamellar armour, their bright pennons and streamers flying in the wind.

They hit the Gothic cavalry in flank. Horses and men vanished under the impetus of their storm-charge, and entire squadrons were smashed to pieces, the survivors scattering in all directions. The bucelarii were supremely disciplined. Instead of pursuing they plunged into the crumbling ranks of Gothic infantry.

I had seen them at work before, at Tricarum, where their repeated charges broke the back and the spirit of the Vandal host. Belisarius had spent much of his personal fortune on their training and equipment, his elite cavalrymen, modelled on the heavily armoured lancers used by the Sassanids in the East. Any one of them was a match for ten ordinary soldiers, and was an expert with lance, bow and sword, as well as a consummate horseman.

As at Tricamarum, I was privileged to watch them from a distance. They tore the Goths apart, slaughtering the hapless infantry like pigs and giving them no respite to rally and re-form. At the same time Belisarius led his personal guard in a counter-attack from inside the Pincian Gate, and the tottering Gothic host was caught between two fires.

By now some of my levies had returned to the standard, though at least half were missing, either dead or plundering the defenceless enemy camp.

"What do we do, sir?" asked my standard bearer. He was just a lad, beardless, fresh-faced and trembling with excitement, and clearly dying to strike his blow.

Hundreds of Goths were fleeing back across the plain, making for the safety of their stockades and entrenchments. They looked like a panic-stricken mob, all discipline and courage gone, their banners and weapons left sprawling in the dust.

I had seen enough of war to know what happened to those who tried to get between fugitives and safety. Even the worst coward can show fight if denied his last refuge.

"We withdraw," I said, ignoring his look of disappointment, "back to the Appian Way."

I gave the order, and led my remaining men west, to rejoin John the Sanguinary.

4.

We caught up with the convoy on the last stage of its journey to Ostia. I reported the news of Belisarius' victory before the gates of Rome, though refrained from mentioning my own modest role in it. A vain man himself, I sensed John was quick to spot vanity in others, and would not give him an excuse to think me arrogant.

"You did reasonably well," he said when I had finished my report, "and it is good to know the general has made our task that much easier. Plenty of Goths killed, eh?"

"Hundreds, sir," I replied, "but merely a drop in the ocean. Belisarius lacks the numbers to inflict a significant defeat on them."

John stroked his carefully oiled and combed whiskers, and gazed west, towards the sea. Our fleet was hugging the coast, on its way to meet the convoy on the southern bank of Ostia. The northern bank, along with the harbour, was still in the hands of the Goths.

We had to devise a way of getting the supplies of corn and wine into Rome. His gaze switched from the west to the convoy, the long, meandering line of ox-drawn wagons lumbering along the highway.

"Those beasts will be done in by the time we get to Ostia," he muttered, referring to the teams of oxen. Our advance was rapid, and the drivers were pushing the animals hard, lashing and cursing them with equal vigour.

To the rear of the convoy, escorted by twenty Hunnish lancers and drawn by a team of white horses, was Antonina's litter. The silk curtains were closed, protecting her from the dust and stink of the convoy. It was all too easy to imagine her lithe form reclining on cushions inside.

Perhaps her new lover Theodosius was lying beside her. I envied the man, without wishing to swap places with him. Only a fool, or one blinded by lust and ambition, would dally with that lethal woman. If Belisarius found out, as he surely would eventually, he would feed Theodosius to his dogs. Usually a merciful man, I had seen Belisarius when his temper was roused, and still shuddered at the memory of the Vandal spy he had impaled on an iron stake outside the gates of Carthage.

The convoy reached the meeting point at Ostia without mishap, to find the fleet already disembarked and three thousand Isaurians encamped along the southern bank. They were in good spirits, though the journey from Constantinople had been long and fraught with danger, and grateful to be on dry land again after months at sea.

John summoned a council in the evening, which all captains were required to attend. No-one invited Antonina, but she came anyway, borne on a divan carried by four sweating Huns. I avoided her gaze, and she never even glanced at me. Her lover Theodosius, young and handsome in the old-fashioned Greek style, with curling fair locks and a neatly trimmed beard, stood behind the divan in a silver helm and cuirasse polished to mirror-like perfection.

Despite his soldierly appearance, everyone present knew what he was, and ignored him. No officer worth his pay was about to heed the suggestions of Antonina's bedmate.

The council had barely started before an alarm sounded, and there was a disturbance to the east: men shouting, horns blowing, and the sound of racing hoofs.

"What's happening, there?" shouted John. For a moment it seemed we had fallen prey to an ambush. A line of torches blazed into view, heralding the arrival of a band of armed riders.

The alarm and consternation died down when their banner became visible, displaying the familiar double-headed eagle of Rome. Under it rode another familiar sight, Belisarius himself, mounted on his white-faced bay. She had carried him through all his campaigns, from Syria to North Africa, Sicily and Italy, and enjoyed almost as much fame as her master.

We cheered the unexpected arrival of our general, but he was in no mood for ceremony.

Lathered in dust and sweat, he wore a plain grey robe over his armour, and the flanks of his shuddering horse were slick with blood. He had a hundred Veterans at his back, hand-picked from his personal guard.

"How many men have you brought?" he snapped at John without exchanging greetings, his voice taut with anxiety.

John was used to more courteous treatment, and blinked before replying. "Ah…five thousand, sir," he managed, "three thousand foot, and two thousand horse. I led the cavalry myself in a forced march across Campania after landing at Otranto…"

Belisarius wasn't interested. "Five thousand!" he yelled, throwing up his hands, "God and the Saints, that is nowhere near enough! Why has the Emperor forsaken me? Have I not served him to the best of my ability? I gave him North Africa, I conquered Sicily without losing a single man, I have defended Rome against the worst that the barbarians can throw at me, and still he denies me the reinforcements I ask for!"

An embarrassed silence fell over the gathering of officers. Belisarius was beside himself, drawn and haggard and thinner than ever, his armour hanging awkwardly off his bony, meatless frame. What he said was almost, if not quite, treason, and there were many listening who might easily twist his words for their own ends.

He must have been desperate to take such an appalling risk, quitting the safety of Rome and riding through the Gothic lines with just a handful of guards. Perhaps he did so in the certain belief that Justinian had despatched a mighty army to save Rome. Grief and disappointment were etched on his face.

Antonina broke the silence. "My lord husband," she said, "the Emperor must have sent every man he could find. There are rumours of plague in some of our provinces, and the imperial treasury is well-nigh exhausted."

He gave her an evil look, narrowing his eyes when he spotted Theodosius, but said nothing. The general's regard for his wife was well-known – indeed, it degraded him in the eyes of many – and even in his rage he would not rebuke or contradict her in public.

"King Vitiges has sent three ambassadors to Rome, asking for a truce," he said, calming a little, "I have granted it. For the present, hostilities have ceased. Hence I was able to ride here tonight."

He turned to John. "I came to urge you to bring your supplies into the city with all speed, while the truce lasts. It must be done now. Tonight. The Goths cannot be trusted, and may betray us at any moment."

John spread his hands. "Now, sir? But our oxen are exhausted, and in any case the only road available to us is narrow and in poor repair. Our wagons cannot travel along it safely at any great speed."

"You have a fleet, man," Belisarius said impatiently, "use boats to transport the supplies."

"But they would have to be towed upriver, sir," replied John, "the only road that follows the stream is on the northern bank, in the hands of the enemy."

I should have known better than to intervene, but wanted to impress Belisarius, and remind him of my presence.

"We could use our sails," I said, stepping forward, "and turn to oars when the wind drops."

John regarded me with disdain. "The Goths will be patrolling the northern bank. Regardless of the truce, do you think they will simply let us sail along the Tiber into Rome? Our crews would have to negotiate a hail of arrows."

An idea struck me. "Then protect the rowers with shields and wooden mantlets. The Goths have no vessels of their own, and can do nothing but shoot at us."

The ghost of a smile appeared on Belisarius' ravaged features. "I should make you a general," he said, pointing at me, "perhaps I will yet."

"I made the Briton a centenar, sir," said John, giving me an evil look, "a temporary command, of course."

Belisarius nodded. "I confirm the appointment," he said, "with all my heart. If only all my officers were so dependable as Coel, and so loyal."

He called for a remount, and changed horses while I gently swelled with pride. I had never craved officer rank, particularly, but it was something to be rewarded for my efforts, and to know I still basked in the general's favour.

I glanced sidelong at Antonina, wondering at her thoughts. Her soft grey eyes briefly rested on me, and then flickered away, their secrets veiled. Theodosius, I noticed, had taken a step back from her divan, and studiously avoided looking at her. That young man, I thought, would soon have to cause to regret stepping into the viper's bed.

Belisarius rode back to Rome, leaving his officers to arrange the transport of the convoy. John wasted no time in rousing the men, ignoring their grumbling and swearing, and ordered them to load the smallest of our boats with provisions.

I was told to oversee the construction of wooden mantlets to protect the rowers.

"It was your idea, *general*," John snarled at me, "and can be your responsibility. If none of our vessels make it to Rome, I will make sure part of the blame falls on your shoulders."

Once again I had succeeded in alienating an important man. Procopius might have remarked again on my talent for making enemies among the rich and powerful, but he had returned to Rome with Belisarius.

The river was narrow and winding, and there was no wind. Our boats rowed through the darkness in single file. John placed me in the first boat, doubtless in the hope that a Gothic arrow would find its way into my gullet.

I stood beside the steersman, shivering in the chill night air and straining my eyes to look for signs of movement on the northern bank.

"They cannot fail to spot us," I muttered. Our vessels were lit by lanterns hanging from the mast-heads, to guard against losing their way in the dark.

The object was not stealth, for there was no way of hiding our progress from the Goths, but speed. Rome had been starving when I left, the citizens forced to eat grass (and each other, if the rumours of what went on in the poorest districts were to be believed) and it was vital our supplies got through without delay.

Occasionally I glimpsed a light on the northern bank, and the dim shapes of horsemen. The Goths were tracking us, but no arrows came flying over the water. The truce was holding.

I learned later how desperate King Vitiges was for a peaceful settlement. Despite being vastly outnumbered, Belisarius had re-conquered much of Italy and defeated all efforts to prise him out of Rome. The Goths were also suffering from famine, for Belisarius sent out frequent raiding parties to disrupt their supply convoys.

With an artfulness that surprised me, he also spread false rumours of the size of the Roman reinforcements about to land in Italy. Had Vitiges known how pitifully few and overstretched the empire's resources were, he might not have been so eager to come to terms.

Even while our boats were rowing up the Tiber, the Gothic ambassadors were striving to persuade Belisarius to abandon the struggle for Italy and accept a compromise. Procopius was present at the negotiations, and told me what passed between the Gothic spokesman and Belisarius.

"My sovereign," said the former, "is guided by the virtues of moderation and forbearance, and sincerely wishes to bring an end to the mutual miseries of this war."

He went on to describe the justice of the Gothic cause, and their legal right to possess the kingdom of Italy, citing dubious precedents from history. Belisarius scornfully denied them all, and then the Goth made this startling offer:

"Though convinced that even our enemies must inwardly feel the truth of the arguments we have urged, yet we are willing to prove our peaceful intentions, by granting you Sicily, that fertile and extensive island, so convenient, by its position, for the maintenance of Africa."

Belisarius laughed at this – he rarely had cause to laugh – and I like to think he had me in mind when he made his reply.

"Your generosity in yielding a province which you have already lost requires an adequate response. I will resign to the Goths the island of Britain, an island much larger than Sicily, and once part of the Empire. May you profit from her!"

The spokesman retreated, red-faced, to hammer out a new set of proposals with his colleagues. Back and forth the negotiations went, and they were still arguing when our fleet arrived safely in Rome.

Our progress down the Tiber had been swift and sure, and entirely without incident. Belisarius was overjoyed at the arrival of fresh supplies of corn and wine, and ordered the dormant mills and bake-houses to set to work again. He was careful to ensure there was enough bread for all, and sent soldiers into the streets to dole out rations to the starving populace.

He summoned me into his presence, at his house near the Pincian Gate, and confirmed my appointment as centenar.

"You have distinguished yourself," he said, clapping me on the shoulder, "as I trusted you would. Coel the Briton, one-time champion of the racetrack, who fought loyally for the Empire and brought the supplies safely into Rome. Soon your fame will eclipse that of your grandfather."

I was surprised he remembered Arthur, whose name was but a faint echo in this part of the world.

"Some of our mercenaries from Germania tell tales of him," he explained, "though they seem to have got him confused with their own heroes. They recite sorts of tales of Arthur hunting a gigantic boar, fighting giants and riding monstrous fish to explore the depths of the ocean. Amusing nonsense, but I am interested in the truth behind it all. He was a great captain of horse, is that not so?"

I nodded enthusiastically. "Yes, sir. His Legion were the greatest horse-soldiers who ever lived. They smashed Britain's enemies in twelve great battles, and held the land safe, without Rome's aid, for over twenty years."

"But Arthur was betrayed and killed in the end, yes? Leaving Britain without a protector."

"That is correct, sir," I replied sadly, "my mother and I fled the country in the aftermath of Camlann, where Arthur's Legion was destroyed. I know nothing of the current state of Britain, whether it has been conquered by barbarian tribes, or split into dozens of warring kingdoms."

Belisarius looked at me for a long moment. He was an expert at concealing his thoughts, and I could only wonder what he had in store for me. With the fate of Italy rested on his creaking shoulders, he must have had good reason to prolong an interview with a nobody like myself.

"Britain has stood alone for too long," he said at last, "it is time all the lost satellites of Rome were brought back into her orbit. We have taken back North Africa, and shall keep Italy, no matter what the Goths throw at us. If we can reconquer Italy, then why not Gaul, or even Britain?"

I stared at him, striving to read his expression. Was he serious? It was impossible. Belisarius had achieved extraordinary things, but to take back the whole of the Western Empire was a dream even Constantine the Great had not entertained. The Empire barely had enough soldiers to defend its own shrunken borders, and the expeditions to North Africa and Italy had been an astonishing gamble. Thanks to good fortune and the skill of Belisarius, the dice had landed in our favour.

And yet…we had watered the soil of Italy with the blood of thousands of Goths, and our own losses were trifling. If all the barbarian nations of the West came against Belisarius, united in arms, I would have given him an even chance of victory.

"Trust in me, Coel," he said with an encouraging smile, "there is no limit to what can be achieved. God has granted us one victory after another. Your homeland may yet be saved."

He said no more, and I left his presence in a daze, striving to make sense of this unexpected glimpse into the general's secret character.

I had never credited him with any ambition beyond carrying out the orders of his master in Constantinople. He might have made himself King of Africa after defeating the Vandals, but declined the opportunity and hurried home to assure Justinian of his loyalty.

Your homeland may yet be saved. These words replayed, over and over again, in my mind that night. I could not sleep, and in the small hours of the morning cursed Belisarius for his vagaries. What had he meant? He was not a man to waste words, or honey them with lies.

Or so I thought.

5

Belisarius was soon active again. He sent John the Sanguinary away from Rome, despatching him north-east with two thousand cavalry to the town of Alba Fucens, beside the shores of the Fucine Lake.

John was instructed to observe the truce and refrain from the slightest act of aggression. If the Goths broke the treaty, he was to ride out without delay and overrun the province of Picenum, a region of Italy between the Appenines and the Adriatic Sea. In this way Belisarius anticipated the renewal of war, and planned in advance while continuing to negotiate with the Goths.

I was happy to see John go, and to enjoy an interval of peace in Rome. The city was still surrounded by a vast horde of Goths, but the morale of our garrison was high, and even the citizens – usually a miserable, cowardly, treacherous set - were buoyed by the recent influx of supplies.

"Give a man enough bread and wine," Procopius remarked, "a woman in his bed, and a chance to score off his enemies, and you won't hear much complaining from *him*."

We had resumed our walks through the city whenever I was off-duty. He delighted in pointing out antiquities and filling my head with the long, complex and bloody history of

Rome. I was happy to listen. Procopius had a passion for teaching and history, and it was easier to succumb to it than resist.

"There," he said, indicating a familiar sight, "the sepulchre of Hadrian. You know it quite well, I believe."

I did indeed. It had been the scene of some of the fiercest fighting for Rome, when the Goths had launched an all-out assault on the walls and chosen the sepulchre as a weak point in our defences. I had helped to repulse the assault, ordering my men to fetch the statues of old Roman gods decorating the terrace, and fling them down on the heads of the Goths. Exposed to a deadly hail of statuary, the enemy had retreated, leaving a number of their comrades crushed like insects under figures of Mars and Jupiter.

"Some of the citizens called my actions blasphemy," I said, "there are those in Rome who still favour the old gods, and would happily abandon Christ. I have seen them, scowling and making the sign of evil at me in the street."

"Madmen," Procopius said with a shrug, "every city has them. Fear not. I imagine the Emperor Hadrian would have approved. He was a practical man."

I paused to study the defences. The space between the sepulchre and the Flaminian Gate was marked by the flow of the Tiber, and the walls along the riverbank were low and unprotected by towers. There were men patrolling the ramparts, but they could have been scaled from outside without too much difficulty.

"The Goths were right to identify this as a weak spot," I said, "Belisarius should strengthen the guard."

"With what?" replied my friend, "even with reinforcements, our garrison is thinly-spread. Rome is a big city, and they have miles of wall to cover. In any case, the spirit of the Goths is broken. Why else would they beg for a truce? One more push will topple Vitiges from his throne."

He was almost correct. The Goths, and Vitiges, were not quite done, and made two last-ditch efforts to recapture Rome.

Disregarding the truce, Vitiges sent a band of chosen soldiers to explore the old aqueducts outside the city walls. They crept into the tunnels at night and levered a piece of stone from the buttress that Belisarius had constructed to guard against just such an entry. The glimmer of their torches was observed by one of our sentinels, but he and his foolish comrades agreed it was nothing suspicious, and probably the eyes of a wolf glowing in the dark.

The Goths took the stone back to their chief as proof of their efforts. Vitiges might have sent them back into the tunnels with picks, to break down the buttress and gain access to the city, but sheer chance foiled his plans: Belisarius happened to overhear the guards talking of the phantom wolf in the night, and sent men to check the aqueduct. They found the discarded torches of the Goths, and the hole in the buttress, and so Belisarius immediately trebled the guard along this stretch of wall.

Frustrated yet again, Vitiges turned to deceit. Even now, after all our victories, there were those among the Roman citizenry prepared to betray their countrymen for a handful of barbarian gold.

Vitiges procured the services of two such traitors, named Cassius and Gaius, and paid them to offer drugged wine to the guards defending the weak section of wall between the sepulchre of Hadrian and the Flaminian Gate.

Meanwhile the Goths obtained some boats and crammed them with soldiers. When the guards on the wall were asleep, knocked out by the narcotic in the wine, Cassius and Gaius were supposed to raise a lantern. The Goths would then cross the Tiber, scale the undefended walls and open the gates to their comrades.

I knew all this because Cassius lost his nerve on the eve of the attempt, and came to my quarters to pour out his tale.

He was a tall, emaciated individual, a butcher by trade, and stank of offal. The stench mingled with the smell of his fear as he knelt before me and clutched at my legs with trembling, clammy hands.

"Please, sir," he babbled, "you must save me. Speak for me with the general – they say he favours you, and you have influence with him."

I had just finished supper, and was alone in the little room I had hired above a wine-shop near the Field of Mars, where my men were encamped.

"Curse the landlord," I growled, thrusting the man back with the heel of my boot, "I told him to turn away strangers. Who in God's name are you, and what do you want?"

He told me, snuffling out the details between sobs and whimpers. I never saw a man so frightened in my life.

"I have a wife and seven children, sir," he pleaded, wringing his bony hands, "my trade has fallen away since this wretched siege began, and I have no money to feed them. I had no choice but to take the bribe. It was that or starve!"

"No-one starves in Rome," I said, looking at him with distaste, "Belisarius has made sure of that. I think you were greedy for gold, but lack the stomach for treachery."

He continued to whine and whimper, like a kicked dog, until I was sick of the sight and sound (and smell) of him. I would have preferred to throw him out into the street, but it seemed his colleague Gaius still intended to go through with the plan. Belisarius had to be alerted.

I took the man by the arm and half-led, half-dragged him through the streets to the general's house. After speaking with the Veterans on the door, who recognised me, I was permitted an audience with their chief.

Belisarius sat and listened in grim silence to Cassius, who made an even more abject display of himself. When he was done, and his words had died away in a gruesome mess of tears and snot, Belisarius continued to sit in silence.

I recognised the signs, and feared for Cassius. Some men rant and rave when they lose their temper, but Belisarius was at his most dangerous like this, quiet and pensive.

He was out of all patience, having spent several days wrangling with Gothic ambassadors who offered him nothing and expected gratitude in return. Besides which, he despised spies and traitors, and they tended to rouse him to uncharacteristic acts of cruelty.

"Take this man," he said, turning to the captain of his guard, "he will lead you to his accomplice, a man named Gaius. Arrest Gaius and bring him to me."

Cassius was spared punishment, for which he was pathetically grateful, and the force of the general's wrath fell on his hapless colleague.

Gaius was arrested at his house and brought before Belisarius. He was given no opportunity to explain himself. His nose was slit, his ears were sliced off, and his trembling, mutilated form bound and gagged and mounted on an ass, which Belisarius ordered driven out of Rome.

The beast and her luckless burden found their way to the Gothic camp and the pavilion of King Vitiges, who beheld the bleeding ruin of his last hope with despair.

Belisarius now regarded the fragile truce as broken, and immediately despatched orders to John the Sanguinary, commanding him to invade Picenum. John proved to be a greater soldier than I could have imagined. He led his cavalry on a swift and brilliant campaign, massacring the Gothic troops in the region and laying siege to the cities of Urbino and Osimo.

Like all our captains, John also had an eye to his own profit, and mercilessly pillaged the countryside we had supposedly come to liberate. At last, with the land behind him thick with corpses and rank with the stench of fire and death, he arrived before the gates of Rimini, only a day's ride from the Gothic capital at Ravenna.

In spite of John's merciless plundering, the natives rallied to his banner, swelling the numbers of his little army. Alarmed by the size of the Roman host, the Gothic garrison of Rimini panicked, abandoning the city and fleeing with all haste for the safety of the capital.

At this point, King Vitiges finally lost his nerve. All his efforts to retake Rome had come to nothing, his capital was threatened by our troops, and his army weakened by famine and desertions. Out-thought and outmanoeuvred by his rival Belisarius, sick at heart from all his defeats and disappointments, he reluctantly gave orders for a general retreat.

After over a year of hard fighting, the Eternal City was once again part of the Empire.

6.

On the morning of the twenty-first of March in the year of Our Lord Five Hundred and Thirty-Eight, one year and nine days after the siege of Rome began, I was shaken awake in my dingy quarters by an excited cavalry subaltern.

"Sir, sir!" he yelled in my ear, disturbing my pleasant dream of silken whores and honeyed wine, "you must wake up, sir, and come with me at once! All officers are summoned to muster by the Flaminian Gate!"

I tumbled out of bed, muttering darkly under my breath, and allowed the subaltern to help me dress and arm in the semi-darkness. He was a native of Spoleto, one of the eager young volunteers who had flocked to join our army as soon as it set foot on the Italian mainland. He served as my trumpeter in the detachment of cavalry John the Sanguinary had given me command of, and wore me out with his spirit and enthusiasm.

It was early in the morning, far too early for civilised men to be up and active. I could hear the sound of distant trumpets ringing through the city.

"What's happening?" I demanded blearily, struggling out of my nightshirt, "have the Goths launched a sudden attack?"

"Far from it, sir!" Lucius panted, his beardless face shining with soap and warlike ardour, "the enemy are in full retreat – they are burning their palisades and fortified camps, and streaming back towards the Milvian Bridge! Oh sir, you must come to the walls and see for yourself, it is a glorious sight. The sky is lit up with fire! We have won!"

His excitement was infectious. I shook away the clouds of sleep and dressed hurriedly, snatching a swig of wine from the jug on my bedside table and a bit of bread for my breakfast.

We clattered down the stairs and into the street, which was full of armed men hurrying towards the Flaminian Gate. Horns and bugles echoed through the city, summoning soldiers to their duty. The citizens were careful to stay indoors, though some of the bravest threw open their upper-storey windows and complained at the noise.

One wretched old woman emptied the contents of her chamber-pot on us, soaking Lucius and splashing my best cloak with urine, but there was no time for recriminations.

We hurried on, to find the square before the Flaminian Gate packed with troops. The gates were open, and columns of horse and foot were filing through it in good order to re-deploy on the wide plain beyond.

"Go and rouse our men," I ordered Lucius, "and fetch them here at once, mounted and ready for battle."

He saluted and rushed away in the direction of the Field of Mars, where my levies were billeted. Some three hundred remained under my command. As a mere centenar, I should not have been in charge of so many, but Belisarius had not appointed anyone else in my stead. Either he forgot to choose a more senior officer, or wanted me to prove my worth.

I hurried past the squadrons of infantry, Isaurian spearmen and archers for the most part, towards a group of mounted officers. Their chief was Bessas, Belisarius' second-in-command, a tough, capable officer with the appearance and general demeanour of a disgruntled hawk.

"Sir," I cried, halting at a respectful distance and ripping off a salute, "what is happening? Have the Goths quit the siege?"

He switched his attention from the marching columns of infantry, and fastened his dark little eyes on me.

"Ah, Britannicus," he said, using the old name Theodora gave me in the arena, "yes, the Goths have packed it in, and we're marching out to wave goodbye. Where the hell are your men?"

I reddened. "On their way, sir. The call to arms took me by surprise."

Bessas grunted. "A good officer doesn't wallow in bed when he hears the trumpet sound. He jumps to it, by God! Still, you're not the only laggard in our ranks. The army is not what it was. When your men finally graces us with their presence, lead them out of Rome and take up position on the left wing, behind the Huns. When the Huns advance, you will support them. Understand?"

"Sir," I saluted again and withdrew, grateful to be spared anything more than a tongue-lashing. Bessas was a fearsome disciplinarian, and made no distinction between officers and men when doling out field punishments.

Our army was sallying out in force, leaving scarcely a man behind to defend the city. Belisarius, who was already outside at the head of the vanguard, meant to pursue the Goths and catch them before they could withdraw across the Milvian Bridge.

Lucius returned with commendable speed, mounted and leading my horse. My men cantered behind him. They were a motley, undisciplined crew, though full of youthful zeal, and I was hard-put to restrain them from pushing ahead of the infantry.

We finally emerged from the gate as part of the rearguard, and I looked for the detachment of Hunnish cavalry on the left wing.

There was no left wing. Belisarius had decided to seize the initiative and order a general advance instead of waiting for his army to lumber into position. With every passing moment, more Goths were escaping across the bridge onto the Tuscan side of the river.

Trumpets squalled across the plain, and a massed roar burst from the leading squadrons of cavalry as they surged into a gallop.

I saw Belisarius' banner to the fore, rippling at the head of his Veterans. As Lucius had said, the sky was on fire, the reddish pink of dawn obscured by twisting pillars of smoke and leaping tongues of orange flame. The Goths had set light to their camp – tents, stockades, wagons, towers and all, hoping that the conflagration would shield their retreat.

Belisarius cared nothing for fire. His cavalry raced in pursuit, leaping the deserted entrenchments and charging through the wall of smoke. They disappeared from view, though the sound of fighting and killing could be heard beyond.

"Charge!" I shouted, drawing Caledfwlch. Lucius sounded the order, and we galloped forward in the wake of the forward squadrons, determined to be in at the death.

The siege had been long and bloody, with no quarter given on either side. Hatred of the Goths spurred on my men, especially the natives, raised on tales of their ancestors and the lost glory of the Western Empire. Here was a chance to throw off the shameful yoke of their barbarian conquerors and reclaim their city.

We careered around a line of burning wagons, and burst through the veil of smoke into a scene of bloodshed. Thousands of Gothic auxiliaries were stampeding towards the bridge, but the foremost of our cavalry had caught them in the open.

The Goths were trying to turn, to form line of battle against our heavy lancers and horse-archers, but everywhere their discipline was failing. I saw Gothic officers, brave men, dismount and rally around their standards, resolved to die fighting rather than show their backs to the enemy.

Some managed to collect enough men to form a semblance of a shield-wall. Our horse-archers rode around them in circles, shooting the hapless Goths down from afar, swiftly eroding their ragged lines until nothing remained but a few wounded survivors and great piles of arrow-riddled corpses.

Belisarius allowed them no respite. His Veterans had ploughed into the rear of a detachment of spearmen, spearing and trampling half their number and sending the rest fleeing in bloody rout.

My men were eager to join the hunt, but I was careful to restrain them. They were light cavalry, armed with shields and spears, and would come to grief if I threw them against the Gothic shields. I had enough experience of war to know that light cavalry are best used as skirmishers on the battlefield, harrying the enemy flanks and hunting down fugitives.

I looked around, and spied a unit of Gothic javelin-men breaking away from the fighting and fleeing along the bank of the Tiber. Some followed the course of the river, others threw away their helms and shields and plunged into the water, hoping to swim across to the opposite bank.

"Ride them down!" I shouted, straining my voice to be heard above the din, "drown them in the river! Kill them!"

I steered my horse to the south, skirting the edges of the battle, followed by Lucius and my standard bearer. A good number of my command followed, though others peeled away to loot the dead and dying.

The Goths tried to run, but my men spread out to herd them down the steep slope towards the river. There, in the shallows, we butchered them at will. Some few offered desperate resistance, others begged for life, falling on their knees in the water and screaming like frightened children.

"No mercy!" I bawled, my sword-arm red to the elbow with barbarian blood, "slay them all!"

I am not a cruel man, but this was war. The Goths still held a massive advantage in numbers, and it was imperative we killed as many as possible. Even now, with half his army in full flight, Vitiges might rally the remainder and overwhelm us.

From the river, I had an unrivalled view of what happened next. Vitiges could be forgiven for thinking he had suffered enough disasters, but God was not on his side.

The King had escaped to the Tuscan side of the river, and there tried to regroup his battered host and launch a counter-attack. His best troops rallied around the royal banner, and stormed back across the Milvian Bridge to aid their comrades being cut to pieces on the other side.

At the same time the wavering Gothic infantry broke under our relentless assaults. Abandoning their standards, they flooded towards the narrow stone bridge. Our triumphant cavalry rode among them, hacking and stabbing, carpeting the ground with bodies.

Before the siege began, Belisarius had constructed a gigantic wooden tower at the eastern end of the river, to guard against the enemy attempting a crossing. The Goths had seized the tower and held it ever since, but now panic seized the garrison. They quit their posts, running down the steps outside the tower or leaping from the parapet into the fast-flowing waters of the Tiber.

Many drowned, or were shot down as they tried to swim to safety. Soon the river was full of floating corpses, gently swirling in circles as they were washed downstream.

I watched, my nostrils filled with the heady stench of blood and death, as the runaways from one side of the river collided with reinforcements from the other. The bridge was too narrow to bear them all, and hundreds of Goths were pitched howling into the Tiber.

Weighed down by their armour, many swiftly sank from view. Others tried to struggle out of their heavy mail hauberks before they were dragged under. I almost pitied the wretches as they floundered helplessly in the water. Some of our men dismounted and enjoyed great sport on the riverbank, shooting arrows and casting spears, until the Tiber was choked with human wreckage.

The Goths on the Tuscan side of the river were powerless to help their comrades. I saw the royal standard start to move away from the field, and briefly glimpsed Vitiges himself under it, a stocky, compact figure mounted on a chestnut mare. His guards closed up around him as he left the field.

"Roma Victor!"

The ancient war-cry echoed and re-echoed across the field. The Goths were beaten, and the victory of Belisarius was complete.

7.

I expected Belisarius to unleash his cavalry and send us in pursuit of the retreating Goths. Instead, ever cautious, he despatched a mere thousand horse under a captain named Hildiger, with orders to shadow the Goths and obtain reinforcements from our garrison stationed at the seaport of Ancona.

Belisarius was right to be careful. A wounded beast is dangerous. The Goths still outnumbered us, even after losing half their army at the Milvian Bridge.

Vitiges fled north, to his capital at Ravenna, and covered his retreat by leaving men to guard certain towns and fortresses. Four thousand at Auximum, two thousand at Urbino, and another three thousand scattered among smaller places.

Belisarius despatched me with Hildiger to track the Goths. Hildiger was a capable and experienced officer of mixed Germanic ancestry, and I was to act as his second-in-command.

"Another promotion," said Procopius, who was present in the general's pavilion, "though an unofficial one. *Pro tem*, as it were. Continue to do well, and you might find yourself in charge of an army."

"In which case, God help the Empire," I replied. Procopius snorted with laughter, but Belisarius was not amused.

"I have no time for false modesty," he said sharply, "we have a war to win. I need officers who are not only loyal and obedient, but confident in their own abilities. Am I right to place my faith in you, Coel?"

"Yes, sir," I replied stiffly. What else could I say? Privately, I suspected him of favouring me for political rather than military reasons, and had not forgotten his words during our last meeting.

Your homeland may yet be saved.

I thought it cruel of him to encourage my dreams, and to make vague promises he had no means of fulfilling. Belisarius had always been honest and generous in my dealings with him. This was out of character. For the moment, all I could do was accept the promotions he foisted on me, and follow his orders.

"From Ancona, you will march with all speed to Rimini," he said, tracing the route with his index finger along a map of central Italy, "avoid the Goths at all costs. Under no circumstances are you to engage them, is that clear?"

"Yes, sir," said Hidilger, "when we reach Rimini, what then?"

Rimini was the city on the shores of the Adriatic, just a day's march south from

Ravenna. John the Sanguinary had taken the place after a brief siege, and now held it with his two thousand cavalry.

"Order John to depart," Belisarius went on, "and use his cavalry to harry the flanks of the Gothic army as they advance towards Ravenna. The soldiers from Ancona will garrison the place. Once this is done, you will return to Rome."

"Coel," he added, looking up at me, "I want you to stay at Rimini, as captain of the garrison. The Goths will do their utmost to retake it. Hold it for me, until I march to your relief."

I tried not to display any sign of nerves. "Yes, sir."

"The general favours you," remarked Hidilger afterwards, as we sat our horses on the Tuscan side of the Tiber and watched our men file across the Milvian Bridge.

It was the morning after the battle, and the river was still choked with bodies. The air was rank with the putrid stench of death and the buzzing of millions of flies.

Hidilger prodded me in the chest. He was a typically thickset German officer, big and blonde and heavy-jawed, and brooked no nonsense.

"If Belisarius rates a man's ability, then I respect his judgment," he grunted, "but get no ideas above your station, you hear? You are my subaltern. Contradict me in front of the men, question my decisions and orders, and I'll take you apart with my fists. Got that?"

"Of course, sir," I replied.

In truth, I knew how to handle men like Hildiger. I had served under Mundus, an even bigger and more intimidating German and a far greater soldier, and done well enough.

We advanced north as Belisarius instructed, following the Flaminian road, and avoided the Goths by swinging east to force a passage through the mountains.

These were guarded by the fortress of Petra Pertusa, but we gave its walls a wide berth and made our way through narrow, rocky defiles, guided by maps and a native shepherd Hildiger had bribed with a handful of silver.

Vitiges was either blind to our presence, or too much in a hurry to reach the safety of Ravenna to care overmuch. A mere thousand horse presented little threat to his army, and he made no attempt to prevent us reaching the sea-port of Ancona.

My relief at laying eyes on the city was tempered by the sight of the military camp spread out on the landward side of its walls. At first I thought another Gothic army had landed in Italy, and was seized by despair, but then I saw the Roman banners fluttering among the neat lines of tents.

"More reinforcements from Constantinople," said Hildiger, "they must be.

Strange. Belisarius made no mention of their arrival."

Mystified, he ordered me to ride down to the camp and seek an audience with their commander. I obeyed, taking six men for an escort.

In fine old Roman style, the camp was surrounded by a ditch and a stockade. I was hailed by the sentinels on the gate. They were Heruls, and I merely had to display the faded tattoos on my right arm to gain their approval.

"I wish to see your general," I cried.

"Welcome, friend," one of them called back, "bring your men inside, and we'll see about gaining an audience."

I led my escort inside, and accepted the wineskin and lump of dry biscuit offered by the guards.

The possible identity of their commander puzzled me. All of Rome's best commanders were already in Italy, or at least those I knew of. I judged there to be at least five thousand men inside the camp, probably more. The Emperor's judgment was not always perfect, but he surely wouldn't entrust an army to some inexperienced officer or court favourite.

Where, for that matter, had Justinian managed to find the men? He had always starved Belisarius of money and soldiers, claiming the Empire's limited resources were already stretched to breaking point.

Belisarius' achievements, given this lack of support, were all the more remarkable.

The Heruls soon returned. "The general will see you," said their captain, "but only you. Your men stay here."

I shrugged, trying not to show my disquiet. "Very well. But I go armed."

The captain made no objection, and took me through the camp towards the large pavilion in the centre. I took careful note of the soldiers, their tents and gear and provisions.

The imperial eagle flew above the pavilion on a tall striped pole, and the walls of the pavilion itself were made of gold and purple silk, a princely bower for an important man to recline while his soldiers slept under rough canvas.

Two tall swordsmen in richly-decorated armour and crested helmets guarded the entrance. They were *doryphori*, elite soldiers trained in Constantinople, better-paid and equipped than the rest of the army. Only very rich men, aristocrats usually, could afford to hire them as part of a private retinue or bodyguard.

The Herul captain exchanged salutes with the guards, and ducked inside the heavy silken folds of the pavilion.

I followed, heart thumping, and found myself inside a miniature palace. A cloying, sickly scent of perfume and incense filled the air. The ground was covered by layers of thick rugs, all of them intricately woven in the Eastern style, displaying twisting patterns of flowers and ovals, diamonds and hexagons, alongside naked humanoid shapes – gods and monsters and men - that seemed to writhe when the eye fell on them.

The carpets were strewn with purple and gold cushions, and the marble busts of four Emperors stood in each corner. Tellingly, they were four of the worst Emperors the Empire had ever known, masters of every kind of cruelty and depraved excess: Caligula, Nero, Caracalla and Elagabalus.

In the middle of this opulent, slightly queasy splendour, was a large divan and an elaborately carved table made of some dark polished wood.

The occupant of the divan smiled at me, and raised his goblet in salute. He was an ugly, crippled, dwarfish eunuch, as corrupt in mind as he was in body.

"Hello, Coel," said Narses.

8.

I stiffened, my hand flying to the hilt of Caledfwlch, half-expecting to feel the sharp kiss of steel in my back. Narses' guards were just outside, well within striking distance.

A high-pitched little giggle came from the divan. "Oh, really," said Narses in that piping squeak I remembered so well, "don't be so jumpy. Do you think I mean to have you killed? How divine."

He wiped his mouth, and mopped at some wine spillage down the front of his loose robe. "If I wanted you dead," he added, discreetly stifling a belch, "you would already be enjoying the company of your ancestors. I imagine you and your grandfather would have a lot to say to each other."

I shuffled away from the entrance, keeping a wary eye on him. He was impossible to trust, the wiliest and greasiest politician in Constantinople, intelligent, devious and merciless. His enemies tended to underestimate him, and made the mistake of judging him by his feeble, stunted form. His enemies tended to die.

Narses was my enemy, or so I thought. The last time we met, in Constantinople, he had demanded I give him Caledfwlch. I refused. Narses was not used to being denied.

He took another sip of wine. "Quite a coincidence, you coming here," he said, "God wants us to be together. I cannot help noticing that I am making all the conversation."

"Perhaps God has sent me here," I hissed, "I could kill you, here and now. Try calling for your guards. I would reach you first."

I half-drew Caledfwlch, exposing several inches of bright steel. Narses' eyes flickered, but his manner didn't change.

"What is all this talk of killing?" he asked, gently placing his cup on the table, "I have an inexhaustible list of enemies, entire ledgers full of names, but had not counted yours among them."

I lost my temper. "You tried to have me murdered in Constantinople! Your assassins laid siege to Belisarius' house while I recovered from my wounds, and then stalked me through the streets. You sent Elene and a treacherous guardsmen to hunt me through the ruins of the aqueduct outside Naples. Only God preserved me from the blades of your hired killers."

My anger was somewhat contrived. I didn't know if he was behind all these attempts on my life, and wanted to draw the truth out of him. Hard experience had taught me a degree of artfulness, though I was never a match for the likes of Narses.

He looked surprised, and even a little hurt. "Dear me," he exclaimed, shaking his ugly head, "it seems there has been a misunderstanding. I bore no grudge against you for refusing to hand over Caesar's sword. After all, it is the most precious thing in the world to you. I merely saw it as an interesting relic."

"As for the various bungled efforts to kill you," he went on, "I did indeed have men watching you in Constantinople, but they were there for your protection. I can only assume Belisarius told you otherwise. Regarding Elene, I would not be so coarse as to send one of your ex-lovers to put you in the ground. No, that was Antonina's doing."

I had suspected as much, but it was good to have my suspicion confirmed. That said, I would have been a fool to place too much faith in his words.

"I see Belisarius has made you an officer," he said, "I am guilty of misjudging him. He is a far more subtle man than I thought."

"What do you mean?" I demanded. If Narses wished to turn me against Belisarius, he was going to have a hard time of it.

"He has made you his ally, showered you with favour and promotions, and succeeded in persuading you that he is your only true friend. All lies, Coel. It seems our golden general is not immune to deceit. I have always been your friend. Did I not rescue you from Theodora's bed of pain?"

I hesitated. It was true Narses had saved me from being broiled alive by the Empress.

"You did it to spite her," I snapped, "rather than any concern for my wellbeing. I will not be poisoned by your venom, snake."

Narses sighed, and ran a hand through his beard. "I cannot do right, it seems. I am accused of being a typical lying politician, and yet when I tell a man the truth he throws it back in my face. Ah, well. You will learn. Belisarius is using you. Shaping you to his own ends."

His squealing voice had an oddly seductive, persuasive quality, but still I refused to listen.

"What are you doing in Italy?" I asked, "why has the Emperor furnished you with an army, instead of sending the troops to Belisarius? You are no soldier."

Narses shifted into a more comfortable position on the divan. "Perhaps not, but I am a reasonably competent chess player. Chess is a game of war, is it not? One moves the pieces on the board, tries to predict the strategy of one's opponent, to outflank and outmanoeuvre him. It has the advantage of being bloodless, though occasionally a game ends in blows."

I almost laughed. It was absurd, the notion of this twisted little half-man leading a Roman army into battle. He was fit for nothing but court intrigues, and should have remained in the lethal warren of the imperial court in Constantinople, where he reigned supreme.

Narses noticed my amusement, and gave one of his lazy smiles. "Seven thousand men, Coel," he said, "the Emperor gave me all the troops he could spare. Why not send them to Belisarius, you ask? Because it is possible to be too successful, and emperors have fallen victim to over-mighty subjects before now. In short, Justinian trusts me, but not Belisarius."

"Then he is a fool indeed," I retorted. I was keen for the interview to end, but at the same time wanted to know the eunuch's plans, and the Emperor's reasons for sending him to Italy without informing Belisarius.

Narses sighed again and sat upright, swinging his short legs over the edge of the divan. "I knew you wouldn't believe me, and that I would have to provide some evidence of my good faith. Like everyone else, you judge me by my appearance and reputation."

I started to mouth a denial, but Narses raised his hand. "Please. I don't blame you. What right-thinking person would believe the words of an abomination like me? I ought to have been exposed at birth and left to die."

"My evidence is this. The woman Elene, your ex-lover, is inside Ravenna. She disappointed Antonina once too often, and threw herself on the mercy of the Goths to escape retribution. King Vitiges has taken her as an agent and a bedmate. She is still an attractive woman, and knows how to snare a king, especially one in such desperate need of comfort."

This shook me a little, but it had a ring of truth. Narses had no conceivable reason to feed me lies regarding Elene.

"I care not where she is," I replied, "or what she does. Elene means nothing to me."

Narses sniffed, and tapped his fingertips together. "She is not alone. Arthur is with her. Her son. Your son."

Silence reigned inside the pavilion while I digested this. The reek of incense was starting to effect me. I felt dizzy and light-headed.

"Arthur is not mine," I managed at last, "she named him after my grandsire to spite me. He is another man's son. A man she married, long after we had parted ways."

"Believe me, Coel," said Narses, "I spoke privately with Elene in Constantinople, and met the boy. She spilled all her secrets in exchange for a bag of gold. Not a very large bag, in truth. She assured me you were Arthur's father. There never was a husband. You were the last man to lie with her."

He picked up the wine jug, wrinkled his misshapen nose in disappointment when he saw it was empty, and set it down again.

"She agreed to work for me, sending me the details of Antonina's private letters, and was useful for a time. When she defected to the Goths, my agents trailed her to the gates of Ravenna."

"Enough of politics," he added, stretching out his right hand, "may I be the first to offer you my belated congratulations, Coel. You are a father."

I stared at his hand, and at the grinning face above it. It was tempting, sorely tempting, to draw Caledfwlch and cleave his skull in half, but his guards would have butchered me on the spot. I had to live, to hunt down Elene and wring the truth from her.

Without waiting for permission to leave, I stumbled out of the pavilion, past his startled guards. They might have barred my way, but Narses' voice squealed from inside.

"Ah, let him go!"

9.

I rode back to Hildiger in a daze, and reported the arrival of Narses.

"Politics," said Hildiger with a grimace, "we have not yet won this war, and already the politicians are moving in. So he told you the Emperor distrusts Belisarius, did he? Perhaps Caesar sent Narses to act as a counter-weight to the general's ambitions in Italy."

I listened distractedly, my mind weighed down with personal matters. The progress of the war was no longer important to me. All that mattered was getting inside Ravenna, and finding Elene. Finding my son.

She had lied to me, all those years ago, in the dungeons under the Great Palace in Constantinople. I had been on trial for my life, falsely accused of conspiring to overthrow the Emperor. Elene came to visit me, in the darkness of my prison, and begged me to plead guilty to save the life of her son and husband.

According to Narses, her husband was a figment of her imagination, invented to manipulate me. Her son…our son…would be about sixteen by now, and had never known his real father. Had Elene never told him about me? Had she poisoned his mind against me, teaching him to hate and despise the man she once loved?

The man she tried to kill, under the ruins of the aqueduct outside Naples. Elene was a traitor, a double agent and a murderess. Like Theodora and Antonina, she had started life as nothing, a mere dancer and prostitute in the Hippodrome, and tried to claw her way out of the gutter. Unlike them, she had failed, and now cowered behind the walls of Ravenna, waiting for the end.

Once the city fell, Vitiges would not be able to protect her. He would be shipped back to Constantinople, to be paraded as a trophy through the streets, before facing execution or lifelong imprisonment.

I almost felt sorry for her. At least she loved Arthur – she must have done, to keep him by her side for so long – though I could only shudder at the thought of his upbringing, and what kind of man he had become.

Hildiger's harsh voice snapped me out of my reverie. "Coel," he barked, "pay attention, man. What does Narses intend to do? Did he divulge his plans?"

I shook my head. "No, sir. He told me very little."

In truth, I had neglected to ask, so desperate was I to get out of the pavilion, but Narses would never have revealed his intentions anyway. He had fed me just enough information as suited his purpose.

The eunuch never said anything without a reason, and in this case he meant to turn me against Belisarius. I was supposed to feel grateful to him, for informing me I had a son, and of Elene's whereabouts.

If Narses had a fault in his dark designs, he tended to over-elaborate. I felt no gratitude, and indeed felt little at all save confusion. I was a simple man, of no great virtue and distinction, and easy prey for those who wished to manipulate me. They shifted me about like a pawn on a chessboard, a useful but disposable tool.

Hildiger rubbed his chin and gazed down at the encampment. "Well, seven thousand extra Roman troops in Italy cannot do our cause any harm," he said, "let's see how many men we can screw out of Narses. Then we press on to Rimini."

Narses proved accommodating, and gave Hildiger five hundred infantry. Our combined force marched north from Ancona (none too soon, in my view) and advanced on Rimini. Hildiger copied Belisarius' strategy, hugging the coast and sending out scouts to guard our left flank and explore the land ahead.

Rimini was an important city, a vital trade port as well as a link between the north and south of the Italian peninsula, and suitably grand. Julius Caesar had made a famous speech to his legions in the Forum of Rimini before marching on Rome, and his successors had adorned the city with arches, bridges and a fine amphitheatre.

I patted Caledfwlch as we rode under the Arch of Augustus, an impressive stone gateway erected by the first Emperor.

Julius Caesar never carried my sword into Rimini. He had left it buried in the skull of Nennius, a British prince, during his abortive invasion of Britain.

"See, your property is in safe hands," I whispered as I rode past a giant statue of the great man in full military regalia, carved in white marble. A chill stole over me, and for a moment I thought his shade was present, gazing at me in stern disapproval.

John the Sanguinary rode out to meet us under the main gate of the fortress. He wore full armour, and the ramparts above his head were lined with archers.

"Still alive, then," said John, curling his lip at me after exchanging lukewarm greetings with Hildiger, "has Belisarius relinquished his command to you yet?"

He spoke with heavy sarcasm, contempt dripping from every word, but I kept my composure. I wasn't about to be lured into an argument by this vain little puppy. He was drenched in perfume, as usual, and stank like a bed of rotting flowers.

"Belisarius commands you to quit Rimini," said Hildiger, "and hand over the fortress to Coel. He will hold it until the general comes up with the main army from Rome."

John adjusted his sword-belt slightly. I could sense the tension in him, under his usual languid mannerisms, and looked up at the archers on the walls. Something was wrong.

"We avoided the Gothic army on our way here," Hildiger went on, as though nothing was amiss, "they are marching up the Via Flaminia in this direction. Vitiges will probably move on to the safety of Ravenna, but leave a portion of his army to besiege Rimini. He cannot afford to leave the city in our hands. Your orders are to take your cavalry and harry his flanks, pick off stragglers and the like. Do anything to slow his advance."

He twisted in the saddle and pointed south, towards the ancient highway beyond Rimini. "They cannot be more than a day's march away. Good hunting."

John didn't move. He had six lancers at his back, all of them fully armed, their faces hidden under mail coifs. Only their eyes peered out of the holes under their corrugated helmets, narrowed and hostile.

"Well, commander," said Hildiger after a pause, "you heard me. Order your men to move out."

Silence flowed a little longer, and then John raised his lance. The men on the walls immediately notched arrows to their bows.

"I like Rimini," said John, "the sea air does me good. I think I shall stay. You, however, must leave. Inform Belisarius that I will hold the city against the Goths."

He had paled a little, and his voice shook, but he was resolute. I had thought him vain and arrogant, but never suspected he might be capable of mutiny.

Nor had Hildiger. The veteran officer went white, and seemed to swell with rage. "My God, what's this?" he yelled, "you refuse a direct order?"

"I do," John replied, more calmly this time, "Rimini is mine. I took it, with the blood and sweat of my men. It is only right I should defend it."

Hildiger gaped at him. "Yours? What do you think you are, some petty barbarian warlord? Rimini is an imperial city, not an independent fiefdom, and you are an officer in the service of Rome!"

"Rome, yes, but not General Belisarius. I follow a different chief."

Hildiger reached for his sword. I saw the archers draw back their bowstrings, ready to shoot him down.

"No, sir," I cried, leaning over to lay my hand on his sword-arm, "draw, and his men will kill you, I am sure of it."

The other man ground his teeth, but let his hand fall way. "You shall answer for this," he snarled at John, "I shall see you stand before a military tribunal. As for those archers, every one of them shall hang for daring to threaten an officer."

John looked complacent now, secure in the knowledge we were powerless to challenge him. "Who knows?" he said with a smile, "perhaps you shall be the ones to stand trial. The game has just begun, my friends. Now, I must beg you to depart, before my patience runs dry."

Hildiger was the sort of man who preferred to die rather than show his back, but there was no sense in waiting to be murdered. We had just a small group of lancers for an escort, having left most of our men camped outside the city, so as not to alarm the citizens.

"He has two thousand men inside the citadel," growled Hildiger as we turned and slowly rode away, "we have just fifteen hundred, and no siege equipment."

"With respect, sir," I replied, "we dare not try and prise him out by force. The Goths will be here soon. How Vitiges would laugh if he witnessed Romans fighting Romans!"

We cantered over the huge, five-arched stone bridge spanning the Marecchia River. Hildiger paused when we were halfway across and gestured at the inscription sculpted on the inner section of the parapet.

"The Tiberius Bridge," he said, "work started on its construction during the reign of Augustus, and was completed under his successor. The Empire was united then, supremely powerful, and capable of great works. Now look at us. A hotchpotch of degenerates and mercenaries, squabbling over the crumbs of Italy."

It was unlike Hildiger to be so philosophical, but something about John's unexpected betrayal had shaken him.

He turned to look back at the rising walls of the fortress, and the imperial flag fluttering over the gatehouse.

"Damn him," he muttered, "what is he up to? I can see no reason for this treachery. It will mean the end of his career. Maybe his life."

"He said he serves a different chief," I reminded him, "I think I can guess who he meant. Narses."

Hildiger mulled this over. "It makes sense," he said, "I seem to recall John and Narses were friends in Constantinople, though a man like Narses has no real friends, only allies. Perhaps they are hatching some conspiracy together."

"To discredit Belisarius," I suggested, "or at any rate, hamper his conquest of Italy. The Emperor has always envied and distrusted Belisarius, and Narses is the Emperor's creature."

Hildiger urged his horse on, and I followed him to the opposite bank. He said nothing more until we passed through the gates of the city. John, I noticed, had pulled most of his soldiers back to the fortress, leaving the city walls lightly defended.

"I think I can trust you, Coel," he said as we jogged back towards camp, "so I shall speak treason in your hearing. Justinian is an idiot. Belisarius is the greatest living Roman general, the greatest since Aetius, and unshakeably loyal. If he had been properly supported, with money and men and provisions, Italy would already be under our heel. We might be contemplating the invasion of Germania by now, or the recovery of Gaul. Instead Justinian chooses to undermine him, and sends rats to chew at the lion's mane."

Your homeland might yet be saved.

Belisarius' words sounded even more hollow now. The re-conquest of Italy was far from complete, and already the shadows of treachery and civil war loomed over the Roman cause.

10.

Having failed to persuade John the Sanguinary to give up Rimini, we returned to Rome via the mountain passes, avoiding the Gothic host as it streamed up the Via Flaminia.

As Hildiger predicted, Vitiges could not afford to leave Rimini in Roman hands, and laid siege to the city. The King of the Goths took personal command of the siege, perhaps to restore his tarnished military reputation in the eyes of his countrymen. He sent half of his army on to Ravenna, where his energetic Queen, Matasuntha, was refortifying the city walls.

Belisarius had not sat idle at Rome. Unaware of the presence of Narses in Italy, he marched north on what he hoped would be a final push, to break the back of Gothic resistance.

For once, he persuaded his wife to remain behind out of danger, and left her in Rome, where she continued her flagrant affair with Theodosius. Somehow Belisarius remained ignorant of her betrayal, or pretended to, though it swiftly became the scandal of the age.

At first all went well for him. Awed by the terror of his name, the cities of Tudertia and Clusium surrendered as soon as his banners appeared outside their gates. The whole of the central Italian mainland was now in his grasp, and the Goths were in full retreat, abandoning their outposts and pulling back north, to try and regroup in the face of Belisarius' remorseless advance.

We found Belisarius at Clusium, where he had halted to plan the next stage of the campaign. He made the basilica in the centre of the city his headquarters, and was busy poring over maps when we arrived, weary and soiled from the road.

"Coel," he snapped, frowning when he saw me, "what are you doing here? Your orders were to stay in Rimini and hold it against Vitiges."

"Christ's death," he exclaimed before I could speak, throwing down the roll of parchment he had been studying, "has the city fallen?"

"No, sir," I replied, saluting, "Rimini is still in our hands. John refused to give it up."

"We tried to remind him of his duty, sir," put in Hildiger, "and he threatened to shoot us down. The majority of his troops were inside the fortress. We had no means of forcing him to relinquish it."

I thought Belisarius would explode with anger, but instead a great weariness came over him. He sighed, and blew out his sallow cheeks, and pinched the bridge of his nose. This was not the first time he had been failed by a subordinate, but outright refusal to obey orders was something new.

"Is it mutiny, then?" he asked quietly, "has John betrayed Rome, and offered his sword to Vitiges?"

"No, sir," replied Hildiger, "at least, I don't think so. He claims to still serve the Empire, but not you."

"What the hell does that mean?"

Hildiger looked meaningfully at me. He didn't care to tell the full story, and so loaded the responsibility (and the risk) onto my shoulders.

I cleared my throat, which was dry as dust from long hours of riding without pause.

"Sir, Narses has arrived in Italy with seven thousand men. He landed at Ancona and made camp outside the city. I – we – suspect that he and John the Sanguinary are in league together."

Belisarius was no stranger to court intrigues and sudden vicissitudes of fortune, but this took him aback. His long, pale features turned an alarming shade of grey, and for a moment he swayed on his feet, like a tree buffeted by storms.

Procopius hastened forward with a chair. Like a man in a dream, Belisarius slowly lowered himself into it. Outside, the bells of the smaller churches and basilicas inside the city started to toll, summoning the faithful to prayer.

"Betrayed," he muttered, clawing weakly at a map of central Italy, "the Emperor has betrayed me. In the very moment of victory, when I have the Goths on the run, he sends the eunuch to slide a knife into my back."

He placed his elbow on the table and rested his forehead in the palm of his hand. His jaw clenched. For a moment I thought he might start weeping. An embarrassed silence fell inside the nave of the basilica. The assembled officers and subalterns studiously avoided each other's eyes.

"John holds Rimini," Belisarius said slowly, staring at the table, "by now, the Goths will have laid siege. He is shut up there, and cannot get out. So we may forget him for the present. Narses is at Ancona, or was. You know nothing of his plans?"

"No, sir," I replied, "I briefly spoke with him, but he said nothing of importance."

Hildiger might have corrected me, but chose to remain silent. Belisarius looked like a man on the verge of breaking. Being informed that his Emperor – the Emperor he had served so loyally and successfully, for so many years, constantly fighting and winning against the odds – had indeed lost faith in him, and sent Narses to poison his glory, might have tipped him over the edge.

Belisarius gathered himself. "So Narses has come to challenge me, has he?" he cried, "to frustrate my plans and feed the suspicions of the Emperor. Well, I shall go to meet him, and make him welcome in Italy. With a helmet on my head, a sword in my hand, and fifteen thousand men at my back!"

He no longer sounded tired, and his voice rose to a shout.

"Italy has witnessed battles between Roman armies before, and shall do so again, if Justinian's favourite dares to stand against me. Let Narses throw in his lot with Vitiges. Let my enemies join against me. I shall chastise them all!"

Seized with new energy, Belisarius ordered his army to break camp and marched that same day. I had never seen him driven by such anger before. He pushed his troops mercilessly, force-marching them north-east, right across the plains of central Italy. Some fifty miles lay between us and Ancona, and Belisarius was determined to snare the eunuch before he could slip away.

The Goths, meanwhile, were left to reduce Rimini at their leisure, and make Ravenna virtually impregnable. I thought it insane that the Romans should allow their enemy such a respite, but it was ever thus: the history of the Roman Empire, and the Republic before it, is littered with destructive civil wars. Julius Caesar himself had to defeat Pompey and other rivals before he made himself dictator of Rome.

Belisarius sent a troop of Huns ahead to look for Narses and his army. They returned with news that Narses had raised his camp at Ancona, and marched south along the coast to the town of Fermo.

"You will have to run faster, little rabbit," Belisarius remarked grimly, "if you mean to elude me. Fermo, is it? Does his fleet await him there?"

No, came the reply, there were no ships in the harbour. Belisarius looked puzzled, but immediately despatched orders for the army to turn east, straight towards Fermo.

Fifteen thousand horse and foot hurried across the countryside, bypassing numerous towns and villages and small farms. Most of the occupants fled in terror at the sight of our banners, but we left their settlements untouched. The army was well-supplied with provisions, and Belisarius kept driving us on at a furious pace.

Fermo is a pretty little town on a hill overlooking the Adriatic coast. It lay on the junction of roads leading to several Roman towns, making it an important strategic location, and had once been the permanent home of the Fourth Legion.

The legion no longer existed, but Fermo was still important, and commanded a spectacular view of the sea and the surrounding countryside. Narses had chosen his new headquarters well, and spotted our advance from several miles off.

He sent a party of officers to greet us on the western road. They were all smiles and good fellowship, and greeted Belisarius like a conquering hero, smothering him with compliments on his recent victories.

Belisarius was having none of it. "Save your flattery," he barked, "and tell me this. Does your master hold Fermo against me?"

Their leader looked shocked. "Against you, general? Why would you say that? He holds the town for you, and for Rome."

"Then he will have no objection to opening the gates, and allowing my troops into the town."

"None, sir. He is waiting to greet you now, and has set aside food and accommodation for your men after their long march."

Belisarius remained suspicious, and marched on Fermo in full military array, as though he meant to storm the place.

However, the gates stood open, and the soldiers on the battlements cheered and blew trumpets in celebration of our arrival.

"If there is treachery here, it is well-hidden," said Procopius, who had managed to snatch a moment away from the general, "watch your back, Coel, and keep that old sword close by your side."

"I always do," I replied.

Our vanguard rode through the streets, with Belisarius at the head, surrounded by his Veterans. He wore his golden parade armour, making him an easy target for any archers lurking on the rooftops, but there were no assassins in Fermo.

Narses was too subtle for that. He received Belisarius at the governor's mansion, and invited him and his chief officers – and me – to dinner. Belisarius brusquely refused and demanded an immediate council of war instead.

"Of course, general," said Narses with one of his bland smiles, "whatever you wish. You are in command, after all."

I expected the council to be a difficult affair, with Narses blocking the designs of Belisarius at every turn, but all went smoothly. Every officer present agreed on the necessity of relieving Rimini, and deplored the folly of John the Sanguinary in refusing to give it up.

Narses attempted to defend the actions of his friend, against those who called for his arrest and trial. "John is young and rash," he said, "and eager to prove his worth. Too eager, perhaps. He was only recently entrusted with a major command, but he has great ability. We should not be too harsh on him."

"Harsh?" shouted Hildiger, "the little turd refused a direct order, and threatened to shoot me into the bargain."

He appealed to Belisarius, sitting at the head of the table. "Sir, are we to tolerate this sort of behaviour from mere subalterns? In the days of Trajan, he would have been flogged to death before the assembled legions. How we have fallen away in these latter days. Leniency breeds insubordination!"

Some cried approval of this, including myself, but Belisarius looked wary. He was already out of favour with the Emperor, and might fall further from grace if he punished John as the man deserved. On the other hand, if he let him off, he risked losing the respect of loyal officers like Hildiger.

He dealt with the issue by avoiding it. "Enough of this wrangling," he said firmly, "our priority is the relief of Rimini. Our combined forces will march on the city and engage Vitiges without delay. I will deal with John the Sanguinary once the Goths are defeated."

"I am not a military man," piped Narses, folding his hands on his little paunch, "but I can count. We have twenty-two thousand men. Even taking their recent losses into account, the Goths still outnumber us over two to one. It seems folly to engage them in the open."

Belisarius regarded him with undisguised loathing. "You think I mean to charge the enemy head-on, like a bull at a gate? I daresay you would derive much amusement from that

– at seeing my head mounted on a Gothic spear, eh?"

Narses looked affronted. "Not at all. I pray for nothing but your continued success. We fight in the same cause, Flavius."

The tension between the two was almost palpable. Belisarius could have broken the twisted little man's neck with ease, but Narses showed no sign of fear. He was in total control, reclining in his specially raised chair and toying with the rings sparkling on his plump fingers.

Every other officer present remained silent, waiting for the game of wills to play itself out.

"Have you any suggestions to make?" asked Belisarius. His words echoed in the high, vaulted roof of the council chamber, where long-dead Roman governors had once feasted until they were sick.

Narses spread his hands. "Not really. Though it strikes me that Vitiges, for all his undoubted valour, is easily fooled. He succumbed to your every stratagem during the siege of Rome."

"Perhaps," he mused, lifting his eyes to the ceiling, "he can be fooled again."

Belisarius eyed him narrowly before responding. "I had something of the sort in mind. Where is the fleet that carried you to Italy?"

"Still docked at Ancona. It was a rough voyage, and the admiral needed time to repair and refit his ships."

"Send a message to Ancona and order the fleet to sail here immediately. We will split the army in three. One shall embark aboard the ships under the command of Hildiger, and sail back up the coast. I shall lead the main body through the Appenines towards Rimini."

He turned and pointed his long arm directly at me. "Coel shall lead the third detachment. These men will march along the Flaminian Way at night, carrying heaps of timber. When you arrive within sight of the Gothic camp, I want you to light fires, as many as possible. The fires will deceive Vitiges into thinking a great army is advancing on him from the south."

There was a faint murmur of approval around the table, though I was also conscious of jealous glares. Belisarius was publicly favouring me again, this time giving me command of a significant portion of his army.

The mere thought filled me with terror. I desperately wanted to refuse, but he had placed me in a situation where I dared not. Decline in front of my fellow officers, many of whom could only dream of such an opportunity? It would have been interpreted as rank cowardice, and an insult to the general.

"Thank you, sir," I said, though my bowels were dissolving, and placed my hands under the table to hide their trembling.

Of all those present, I believe only Narses guessed my true feelings. I was unwise enough to glance at him, and he gave me a sly wink.

"We shall close on Rimini via land and sea," said Belisarius, "Hildiger, when you see the fires lit, you will disembark and attack the Gothic camp from the east. At the same time I will lead an assault from the south. Coel will advance in support. If John the Sanguinary is half the soldier he pretends to be, he will see the battle in progress and sally out with his cavalry. The Goths may have the numbers, but they lack discipline and composure. When they realise they are caught between four fires, panic and confusion shall do our work for us."

"Another great victory for Rome!" squeaked Narses, clapping his hands together, "I salute you, general, and all your brave officers."

He filled his cup and raised a toast, to which all reluctantly responded. My cup shook in my hand, and the wine tasted like sourest vinegar.

11.

None of his captains would serve under me, so Belisarius despatched Procopius to guide my steps and ensure I did nothing foolish. The general's secretary was no soldier, but intelligent and learned, and had learned something of war from following his master on campaign for so many years.

My detachment was mostly light cavalry, with an infantry escort for the wagons carrying piles of dry timber, hay and brushwood. We advanced after nightfall, following the Flaminian road that eventually arrived at Rimini.

To the east, the lights of our fleet glimmered in the darkness. The ships carried two thousand men under the command of Hildiger. Belisarius had left before me, taking his fifteen thousand east, towards the ridge of the Appenines.

I rode at the head of our column, feeling foolish and overdressed in my fine armour.

"A general must look the part," Belisarius had remarked, and insisted on supplying me with a gleaming lamellar cuirass, a conical helm with cheek-plates, a red cloak trimmed with rabbit fur, and a round shield displaying the Roman eagle. He even gave me a horse from his own private stock, a pureblood black stallion from Hispania.

"I would offer you a new sword as well," he said with a grin, "but nothing on earth will persuade you to part with that relic at your hip."

"Nothing on earth," I agreed, gripping the worn ivory hilt of Caledfwlch. The general's eyes rested on it for a moment. I thought I detected a spark of desire in them, but then he looked away.

My orders were to advance slowly, giving Belisarius time to reach the Appenines and make his way through the rugged mountains towards Rimini. The lighting of the fires was to coincide with his appearance before the walls and Hildiger's seaborne assault from the west.

Procopius rode by my side. He was a born clerk, and looked ridiculous in his borrowed helmet and buckler.

I nodded at the spatha, a long-bladed sword, dangling awkwardly from his hip. "Do you know how to use that?" I asked.

He shrugged his narrow shoulders. "I have watched many a battle. The principle is simple enough. I hit the enemy with my sword, and try and prevent him from hitting me in return."

In spite of my nerves, I had to smile. "Look," I said, pointing at the spatha, "it is heavier at one end and has a sharp chopping edge. You cut down with the edge. Let the extra weight do the work. Don't put your whole strength into the blow, else you may wrench your shoulder. God help you if you miss."

"Noted, with thanks," he replied, "but you need not fear for me. When the fighting starts, I shall take my accustomed place at the rear. Someone has to write down the account of your heroic exploits."

I looked ahead, into the veil of night, and shuddered. The Flaminian Way passed through a range of hills with mountains to the east. Somewhere beyond the mountains lay Rimini.

Like a good little soldier, I had sent men ahead to spy out the land, and look for any Goths waiting in ambush. The greater part of the enemy host, according to Belisarius' scouts, was concentrated around Rimini.

They had the city in a vice, though so far John the Sanguinary had repelled all their efforts to take the place by storm. He led numerous sallies from the walls, slaughtering hundreds of Goths and burning their siege-engines.

I had no cause to love John, but he was a brave and capable officer. A better soldier than me, certainly, though I had the virtue of loyalty.

Loyalty was of little use in my present situation. I could feel the crushing pressure of leadership and responsibility weighing down on my shoulders like a millstone. My thoughts were clouded with a host of fears and uncertainties, and I found it difficult to think of anything save my long-lost son in Ravenna.

In short, I was not fit to command, and was terrified lest I fail Belisarius.

"Why do you think John refused to hand over Rimini?" I asked Procopius, desperate to take my mind off Arthur, "do you think he is truly in league with Narses?"

Procopius pursed his lips and thought for a moment. "They are friends, I know that much," he replied, " but it is impossible to say much more. Spying on Narses is like trying to punch mist. I suspect John acted on his own volition, which is why Narses was so co-operative at Fermo. He wants to drag his friend out of danger, and needs Belisarius to help him do so."

"Belisarius thought Narses had come to Italy to fight him. He marched on Fermo expecting a battle."

Procopius sniggered. "Never. Narses cannot match Belisarius as a general, and was outnumbered two to one. He has his own game to play."

"He told me he was a reasonable chess player."

"An expert. I was fool enough to sit down to a game with him once. My king was slaughtered almost before I could blink. Now the whole of the Italian mainland is his chessboard."

Our conversation died away as we neared Rimini. The lights of the city soon became visible, twinkling like stars, and around it the greater constellation of the enemy camp.

I called a halt, and ordered the first of our beacons to be laid on the summit of the hills flanking the highway. It was a warm summer's night, and thankfully there was no hint of wind or rain.

While the beacons were laid, I sat in silence on the road overlooking the city, nervously chewing my bottom lip until it bled. My scouts returned unscathed, to report no sign of any Gothic outriders.

"Vitiges is neglectful," said Procopius, "even after all his defeats and reverses, he has learned nothing."

"Thank God," I said.

We didn't know it, but there was good reason for the lack of enemy activity. Far from being neglectful, Vitiges had sent out a strong detachment of cavalry to patrol the land south of Rimini and forage for supplies. They advanced too far, and in the darkness blundered into Belisarius' vanguard as it emerged from the Appenines. While I sat and chewed my lip, a messy battle was being fought to the west.

Belisarius charged up in time with the main body, and after a hard right the Goths were routed, leaving a roughly equal number of dead and wounded strewn about the road.

The survivors fled back to their camp, where they tried to excuse their defeat by spreading panicky rumours of the size of the Roman host bearing down on Rimini from the mountains.

Luck counts for a great deal in war. At about the same time as panic was spreading through the Gothic camp, my men lit the beacons. The timber burned beautifully, and within moments the hills over the city were illuminated by two rising columns of flame.

"Light the torches," I commanded. Every man in my detachment carried a torch or lantern, and now set fire to them.

The beacons were swiftly joined by hundreds of lesser lights. I ordered my cavalry to spread out along the ridges either side of the road. To the Goths below, it must have seemed as though the hills were on fire.

At this crucial moment, I was again seized with indecision. My orders were to advance at the same time as Belisarius and Hildiger, but I had no way of knowing their progress. I looked east and west, straining my eyes to make out any sign of my allies, but there was nothing. The mountains hid the fleet from view, and darkness shrouded the Appenines.

"You cannot linger," Procopius whispered, "be decisive, and go forward."

"Five thousand, against forty thousand Goths?" I hissed through gritted teeth, "what if the others fail to support our attack? We would be massacred."

"Better dead than disgraced. You have no choice, Coel. Stop dithering. Advance."

I drew Caledfwlch and kissed the cold steel. It was blasphemous, but I was convinced my grandsire's soul resided inside the blade: neither Heaven or Hell could possibly contain such a fierce spirit.

Shaking off my fears and indecision, I gave the order to advance. My cavalry re-formed on the highway and moved forward at a slow trot, holding their torches aloft.

The city was still some five or six miles distant. As we advanced, I kept my eyes fixed on the enemy camp. There were lights moving down there, and at first I feared the entire Gothic host was marching out to engage us.

If so, I resolved to withdraw. Personal honour was all very fine, but I preferred to live with disgrace rather than the guilt of leading hundreds of men to their deaths.

Hope flared inside me as I saw the lights disperse and scatter away from Rimini in all directions. The sound of distant war-horns reached my ears, booming across the countryside.

I gripped Procopius' arm. "Belisarius," I said hoarsely, "and listen, there, to the east…Hildiger, it must be!"

Our forces were converging on Rimini, exactly as planned. I urged my men on at the canter, all my doubts and fears blown away.

War-delight coursed through me, the strange excitement that seizes men on the verge of battle, turning cowards into heroes. When the fighting is over, the feeling ebbs, and they are left wondering at their own savage excesses.

There was no battle. The Goths had panicked at the sight of our fires, as Belisarius predicted they would, and immediately raised the siege. Thousands streamed north, riding for Ravenna as fast as their horses could carry them, while the infantry were left to shift for themselves.

I rode into the deserted encampment, to find the forces of Belisarius and Hildiger already present in the city. The citizens had thrown open their gates to admit our troops, and the night sky echoed to the thunder of church bells.

John the Sanguinary had remained inside Rimini until he was certain the Goths were retreating, and then unleashed his cavalry to plunder their baggage train. He took prisoners from among the wounded and the stragglers, and made a present of them to Belisarius, hoping to soothe the general's wrath at his treachery.

Belisarius was not the sort to be won over by such crude bribes, but he let John go unpunished. Instead, while his officers were still distracted by the celebrations, Belisarius quietly dismissed him, and let him depart from Rimini with a small following.

Whether he did this for political reasons, or to avoid casting a shadow over the joy of his easy victory, I cannot be certain. There were those who grumbled at it, and looked askance at the general, wondering if he was losing his grip on affairs.

Narses had not marched with any part of the army, claiming that he was quite useless in war, and would only hinder the cause. The morning after the relief of Rimini, he arrived at the gates carried in a litter and escorted by eighteen of his *doryphori*.

"So this is war," he piped when I greeted him at the Arch of Augustus, "it seems a rather bloodless affair. I have seen more casualties in the Hippodrome."

He sounded disappointed, and fanned himself with a fly-whisk. "A foully hot day," he said, stifling a yawn, "I long for a cool bath and a massage. Where is our conquering general?"

"In the fortress, lord," I replied, "where he awaits your arrival."

"Another council of war? How trying. No sooner do we win one battle, then we must start planning the next. I dislike being made to work."

His bored manner was an illusion. All the while his agile mind was churning out schemes to foil Belisarius and discredit him in the eyes of the Emperor.

Belisarius was keen to follow up his victory and stamp out the last embers of the Gothic presence in Italy. The citizens of Milan, capital of Liguria, had recently revolted against the Goths in favour of Rome, and driven out the garrison. Vitiges could not afford to lose one of the most important cities in northern Italy, and sent part of his army to besiege it.

At the council in Rimini Belisarius announced that the army would split in two, one part to besiege Ravenna, the other to relieve Milan.

"I have already sent a thousand cavalry to encourage native resistance in that region," he declared, "but more troops are needed to invest the city."

Narses chose this moment to show his hand. "Milan is far to the north," he said, "I see no reason to divide our forces, slender as they are, and send one part on some hopeless sortie. Let Milan fend for itself. When Ravenna falls, all the Goths in Italy will lay down their arms."

All eyes turned to the eunuch, who revelled in the attention. "Of course," he added complacently, "if Belisarius wishes to send some of his own troops away, that is his affair. But none of my seven thousand shall go with them."

White-faced, Belisarius scraped back his chair and rose to his full, impressive height. "Are you denying my authority?" he asked in the steely tone I had come to know and dread.

"Not within its proper limits. You have no authority over the troops I brought to Italy. They are mine."

Belisarius seemed to have expected some form of resistance. He gestured at Narses, who rose and produced a sheet of vellum from inside his robe.

"This," he said, brandishing the vellum, "is a private letter sent by the Emperor to Belisarius. It reads as follows. Hearken to the words of Justinian."

He unfolded the letter and read out its contents in ringing tones.

"In sending Narses, our private treasurer, to Italy, we have no intention that he should, in any degree, control or direct the war; we desire that Belisarius should still remain invested with supreme authority, and be implicitly obeyed in all his undertakings for the public good."

The letter bore the imperial seal, and there could be no doubt as to its authenticity. I was surprised and encouraged by it – evidently the Emperor still retained some faith in his general – and looked eagerly at Narses. There was no denying an imperial mandate, and it would be a pleasure to witness a hole bored in the eunuch's insufferable complacency.

I should have known better. The subtle mind of Narses had been honed in the deadly intrigues of the imperial court. It took him mere seconds to pick a flaw in the mandate.

"I am perfectly willing to obey Belisarius in most things," he said mildly, "but must, in all conscience, avail myself of the concluding clause in the Emperor's letter."

He spread his hands. "Caesar orders that Belisarius must be obeyed in all his undertakings for the public good. I regard the proposed expedition to Milan as not conducive to the public good. Indeed, it is potentially disastrous to our cause. Therefore no Roman officer, of which august body I consider myself a humble and unworthy member, is obliged to obey his orders in this instance."

Silence fell over the chamber while Belisarius digested this extraordinary response.

He banged his fist on the table. "You dare to quibble!" he shouted, glaring at Narses as though he meant to throw the little man from his seat, "I would remind you this is a military camp, not a law-court, and I will have my orders obeyed!"

Narses matched him stare for stare. "Not, at the danger of repeating myself," he trilled, "in this instance."

They argued back and forth, but Belisarius lacked the means to force Narses into obeying orders. He dared not lay hands on the Emperor's favourite, or take his command away from him. In the end he was obliged to concede, humiliated before his staff, and tear up his plans.

While our commanders argued, Vitiges had not been idle in Ravenna. His armies were battered and depleted after their recent misfortunes, but he was not done yet. Taking advantage of our hesitation at Rimini, he sent messengers racing through the Alps to beg for aid from their kinsmen in Gaul.

"I hope none of you are entertaining thoughts of home," Belisarius said to a gathering of his officers one morning in late summer, "for we are likely to be here some time yet, maybe into the next year."

He looked grimmer than ever, and withered our groans with his basilisk stare. "Last night I received word from our men in Perugia. Vitiges has despatched an army under his nephew, Uraias, to drive our troops from that province."

"Uraias is a pup," Hildiger said scornfully, "send me north with a few thousand men, sir. I'll whip him all the way back to Ravenna."

"I have no doubt you could," replied Belisarius, "but he is not our only concern. Three days ago, ten thousand Burgundian warriors crossed the Alps into Perugia. By now they will have joined the Goths outside the walls of Milan."

"We have much more killing to do," he added during the stricken silence that followed, "before this war is over."

12.

The campaign dragged on into winter. Frustrated and hampered by the machinations of Narses, Belisarius was unable to strike a death-blow against his enemies, and Vitiges was able to recover some of his strength.

Reinforced by the Burgundians, his nephew drove our hopelessly outnumbered forces from Perugia and laid siege to Milan. Vitiges continued to dig in at Ravenna, and despatched men to garrison and fortify a chain of fortresses running down the spine of central Italy, down to Orvieto, almost within sight of Rome.

Belisarius was obliged to reduce every one of these fortresses, as well as other stubborn Gothic outposts scattered about the country. He got little help from Narses, who remained at Rimini, stuffing himself with figs and hatching fresh plots with his friend, John the Sanguinary.

At last, in the depths of December, the main part of our army laid siege to Orvieto, a massive fortress town a few miles north of Rome. It was built upon the flat summit of an isolated hill made of volcanic tuff, with steep, almost vertical sides making it inaccessible from all sides. The natural defences of the tuff cliffs were reinforced by high walls and strong towers, and the town was manned by thousands of Goths.

Confident in their lofty position, and well-supplied with grain, the garrison refused all demands to surrender. For weeks we sat and shivered at the foot of the cliffs, while our siege engines lobbed rocks at the flinty walls, and the Goths responded with showers of javelins and curses.

All the while I thought of Ravenna, and Arthur. I seemed destined to get no closer to either.

One frosted morning I was sat outside my tent, sunk in misery as I tried to warm my chapped hands over a fire, when Procopius strode into view.

"The general wants to see you," he whispered, his breath misting in the cold air, "hurry along, in God's name, before my blood freezes over."

Procopius was a creature of warm climes, and always suffered in the cold. Despite being wrapped up in several layers of shawls over a fur-trimmed hooded mantle and robe, his lips were blue, and his teeth chattered.

I followed him to the general's pavilion, where Belisarius was bathing his feet in a bowl of steaming hot water. He had picked up a cough, and was attempting to drown it in spiced wine.

"Coel," he said, peering up at me from his cup, "you look well. The healthiest man in the army. You Britons must have iron constitutions."

"Our island is foggy, raw and damp, sir," I replied, "we are raised to endure cold. It's the heat I struggle with."

He broke off into a fit of violent coughing. "Damn this chill," he spluttered, wiping his eyes and banging his thin chest, "and damn this siege. Why can't the Goths simply accept they are beaten, and sue for peace?"

"They are a proud race, sir," said Procopius, "Vitiges is the proudest of them. He won't be beaten until you have him in chains."

Belisarius flapped a hand at him. "Never mind Vitiges. I didn't summon you both here to talk of him. Read this."

He picked up a tattered, water-stained letter and shoved it Procopius, who unfolded it and read silently, his bony brows knitted together.

"God curse him," he said quietly, handing the letter to me, "and consign his twisted soul to Hell."

I read but slowly, and had to pick through the words with my index finger. The content was chilling enough.

Milan had fallen. Belisarius had written urgently to Narses at Rimini, pleading with him to send troops under John the Sanguinary to relieve the siege, but the eunuch had demurred, claiming that John had fallen sick with fever.

With no relief on the horizon, the Roman governor of Milan, Mundilas, had surrendered to the combined army of Goths and Burgundians.

"Mundilas obtained terms for himself and his soldiers, but none for the citizens," I read out, "the barbarians sacked and destroyed the city, slaughtering all the men they could find and taking the women and children as slaves. The bishop, Datius, escaped, but the prefect was captured and thrown into a cage full of wild dogs. The animals tore him into pieces and devoured him. Every church was plundered and fired, and the priests themselves massacred at their altars."

I folded the letter, unwilling to read anymore. "If there is one consolation," said Belisarius, "the loss of Milan means the end for Narses. I have already written to the Emperor, complaining of the eunuch's failure to send men to relieve the city. Justinian will surely recall him to Constantinople, and I will be left with a free hand in Italy."

"You may be sure Narses has also written to the Emperor," said Procopius, "putting his own side of the story, and doing his best to blacken you. He is high in favour at court. I fear Justinian will put more faith in his account."

Belisarius winced, stifling another cough, and bade us both sit down. "You two are my friends," he said, "my real friends. The only ones I can trust. I will tell you something now, and want it to remain a secret between us. Understood?"

I exchanged glances with Procopius, and we both nodded obediently.

"Good. Procopius, you are usually the first to know my secrets, but not in this case. For weeks now, I have been in correspondence with Matasontha."

Mathasontha was the Queen of the Goths, and consort to Vitiges. It seems they were not a very faithful or loving couple. She responded to his many infidelities by sending treasonable letters to the Romans.

"She has made me all kinds of offers," he went on, "anything to put an end to this war, to her advantage of course. I will not bore you with the details, save to mention that she even offered to murder her husband and take me in his stead."

He smiled bleakly at our shocked expressions. "A tempting offer, to enter into matrimony with a barbarian murderess. It would also require me to dispose of my poor wife. I refused, as gracefully as I could manage."

I wondered what Antonina would have made of it, and whether Belisarius yet knew of her adultery. If so, he could have put her aside and wed Matasontha, but he loved his appalling wife far too much to even contemplate such a thing. Every great man has a failing. Antonina was his.

"The time will come," said Belisarius, "when the whole of Italy is reduced, and we can finally march on Ravenna. I know that city. She is virtually impregnable, and it would take months, years even, to reduce her by siege and blockade. If I can induce Matasontha to betray Vitiges, and open the gates without a fight, so much the better."

"So far my messengers to her have proved loyal, but they are mercenaries. Hired men, who work for gold. None of them has any love for me. I believe you do, Coel."

I blinked. Belisarius was staring intensely at me, as though willing me to agree. "I am loyal until death, sir," I blurted out, unable to think of anything better."

He nodded. "I know. For that reason I have promoted you, well above what some may regard as your natural station. For that reason I will use you as my envoy to Matasontha. You have never failed me yet."

It sounded like dangerous work, but as always I was in no position to refuse. I bowed my head in acceptance.

"No-one else must know I am in contact with the Goths," he said earnestly, "some of my captains would call it treason. Others would use it as an excuse to undermine me. Our ranks are riddled with traitors and conspirators."

He dismissed me, promising I would be despatched on my first mission very soon. In the meantime I would go about my normal duties and guard my tongue. I left him talking in hushed whispers with Procopius, feeling more like an expendable pawn than ever.

Belisarius got what he wanted. Even Justinian could not ignore the disastrous loss of Milan, and as winter drew to a close he recalled his favourite to Constantinople. His friend John the Sanguinary was recalled with him, and I entertained hopes they might be exposed to the Emperor's wrath.

Narses could not be snared. He managed to clear both their reputations without too much difficulty, and resumed his duties as imperial treasurer, devoting his energies to enriching himself at the expense of the state.

Free of this hindrance, Belisarius' old energy and purpose returned in a flood. Orvieto fell at last, starved and battered into submission, and he flung himself into the task of reducing the remaining Gothic citadels.

I followed him through all the long, wearisome sieges that followed. Our army trudged from one stubborn fortress-town to the next, smashing aside the Goths and their allies when they tried to oppose us in the field. By now, after almost two years of constant warfare, the Roman army was a disciplined and effective war-machine, almost fit to be ranked alongside the illustrious legions of old.

Then the hammer-blow fell. At the beginning of summer, when it seemed the tottering Gothic cause was beyond hope of recovery, terrifying news sped down from Liguria.

"Two hundred thousand," Belisarius said dully, "twice the number of men Vitiges brought to lay siege to Rome."

There was a dreadful, flat quality to his voice, a tone of almost careless despair. He had survived everything fate and his enemies could throw at him, and come within a whisper of final victory, but at the last God had deserted the Roman cause.

The frantic, last-ditch diplomacy of Vitiges had borne fruit. Theodebert, King of the Franks, had brought a vast army over the Alps to join with the Goths and Burgundians in Liguria. The Franks were a numerous people, and their mighty host rolled through the snow-capped mountains like an avalanche, into the fertile plains beyond.

Belisarius looked sick at the news. The council of war he had hastily summoned was a decimated gathering. Almost half our officers were dead, slain in the never-ending series of battles and sieges.

"If these reports are true, we can't fight such an army," croaked Bessas, a dried-up, wizened shell of the man he had once been, "we must ask for peace, and hammer out terms with Vitiges."

"We can fight them. We will. We must." said Belisarius in the same lifeless tone. "The Franks are even more undisciplined than the Goths. Do not be dismayed by their numbers. They have few cavalry, save their king and his attendants, and their infantry are peasants, poorly-armed and trained."

"Two hundred thousand peasants are a formidable prospect," said Bessas.

"I have heard disquieting rumours of their axe-men," added Hildiger, "they carry double-edged battle-axes, capable of cutting a horse and rider in two with one blow."

The news of the Frankish invasion had dealt a severe blow to morale, and Belisarius was unable to raise the flagging spirits of his officers. I said little during the meeting, but was again summoned to his presence afterwards.

"I can't trust any of the others to deal with the Franks," he said, "they are broken reeds, all of them. Even Bessas."

He had shaken off his cough, but still looked ill and tired, and trembled slightly as he faced me. "The Franks cannot be allowed to advance unchecked through Liguria. Even now Theodebert is moving towards the River Po. I have troops there watching his progress, but they are far too few to bar his passage."

I could guess what was coming next, and braced myself. "Six thousand men are all I can spare. I cannot go north myself until

Osimo has fallen, so a trusted subaltern will have to lead them against the Franks."

"I thought you wanted me for an envoy, sir," I said weakly.

"So I do, Coel, so I do. But this present crisis must be dealt with first. Push back the Franks, and Rome will heap you with honours. I will make sure of that. The Emperor will reward you with a triumph in Constantinople, as he rewarded me after the conquest of Africa."

I was tempted to say the Romans would be honouring a corpse, but it would have done me no good. Through my own caution and unwillingness to stand up to the general, I had earned his absolute trust. Now he was relying on me to defeat a massive invasion of Frankish warriors, led by one of the most ruthless barbarian kings of the age.

Just how ruthless, I was about to discover.

13.

My little army marched north into Liguria,
towards the region of the Po where the vast
Frankish horde was said to be massing.
Belisarius was aware of my friendship with
his secretary, and sent Procopius with me.

"He said I am a lucky talisman," said
Procopius, "no Roman army has tasted defeat
while I was present."

"It must be down to your skill at arms," I
said drily. I had watched my friend practising
with the spatha, and narrowly avoid cutting
his own foot off.

"You have never seen me fight in earnest,"
he retorted, shaking his skinny fist, "just wait.
The Franks shall flee before me like fire.
Theodebert will beg for mercy before my
flashing blade!"

Procopius strived to keep up my spirits as
we neared the town of Pavia. Our scouts had
reported the presence of our cavalry near the
town, as well as a squadron of Goths. Both
sides were watching the Franks on the other
side of the river.

It was difficult to predict Theodobert's
intentions. He had crossed the Alps in
response to his kinsman Vitiges' pleas for aid,
but he was a greedy, self-serving warlord,
always with an eye to his own profit. His
army was big enough to crush all of us –

Goths, Burgundians, Romans – and seize Italy for himself.

We were still some miles from Pavia when his motives became clear. A troop of horsemen came flying down the highway in wild disorder, straight towards our vanguard.

"They are ours," I said bleakly, shading my eyes to make out their banners, "Huns, I think. Looks like they have taken a beating."

I counted eleven riders. A few horses with empty saddles trailed behind them. The fugitives had no way of going around us, and so ploughed to a halt in a storm of dust and confusion.

"Well?" I demanded when their shame-faced captain trotted forward. His helmet was gone, his mail hauberk smeared with blood, and his eyes had a familiar haunted quality: those of a man who had witnessed slaughter, and barely escaped with skin and soul intact.

He cleared his throat, and saluted. "The Franks have crossed the river, sir," he croaked, "they fell upon us without warning. We tried to make a stand, but there were too many. They attacked the Goths as well, and drove them back towards Ravenna."

Procopius gave a low whistle. "So Theodobert has betrayed his ally. What faithless scum these barbarians are. Then again, why not? He has enough men to defeat all of us."

"What of their numbers?" I asked, trying to suppress the rising tide of panic in my breast, "is the Frankish host as big as they say?"

The captain ran a shuddering hand over his face. "Yes, sir. Like a plague of locusts, covering the land as far as the eye can see. Nothing but banners, and hordes of barbarian warriors, filling the air with their accursed chanting…"

He was clearly a broken man, and I dismissed him to the rear with what remained of his command. I beckoned at Procopius to ride a little way forward with me, out of the hearing of my subalterns.

"What should I do?" I hissed, "I can't offer battle against such a horde. What do you know of this Theodobert? Is he a better soldier than Vitiges?"

Procopius nodded grimly. "A better soldier, and a shrewder and greater man in all respects. He won't be fooled by our paltry war-tricks, as we fooled Vitiges at Rimini. Theodobert is a wolf, and will tear our throats out if we let him."

He glanced at the barren fields beside the highway. They were untilled, the peasants who usually worked the land either dead or driven off. No crops grew on the parched soil, where there should have been a ripe yield of golden corn.

Vast stretches of the Italian countryside were equally afflicted, the natural rhythms of the seasons disrupted by the ravages of war. As a result, thousands of peasants were condemned to starve, or swell the numbers of beggars in the towns.

"We can't fight the Franks," Procopius said softly, "but we don't need to. Nature can fight them for us."

I took his meaning. The Frankish host was enormous, and would have to live off the land. Thanks to the poor harvest, there was precious little for them to take. In time, hunger and famine would achieve what our swords could not.

I ordered the retreat, back towards the nearest Roman garrison at Fiesole, a fortified hilltop town inside Tuscany. The walls were strong and well-maintained, and I counted on being able to hold the place against a siege.

There we awaited the onset of the Franks. Liguria was now laid open to them, and they devastated the region with typical barbarian savagery, carrying fire and slaughter to all corners.

Uraias abandoned the province, fleeing back to his uncle at Ravenna with his remaining troops. Exulting in his conquest, Theodobert picked Liguria clean, though he found little to please him in the burned and blackened ruins of Milan.

The summer of that year was unforgiving. A heat haze settled over the land. Nothing grew, and such scanty crops as had been planted withered and died in the fields. The dreaded but inevitable spectre of famine stalked the countryside, bringing starvation and the bloody flux to the country folk.

"The Franks will also be suffering," said Procopois as we stood together on the walls of Fiesole one evening, watching the blood-red sun dip below the hills, "Theodobert will have to break up his army, or lose it."

I sent out riders to observe the enemy, and they brought back encouraging reports. The Franks were indeed suffering. Desperate for food, they had stormed and ransacked every settlement they could find, butchering the inhabitants and – if some of the more lurid accounts were to be credited – occasionally eating them.

The news brought me little joy. Belisarius had entrusted me with the task of driving the Franks from Italy, but instead I had taken refuge behind high walls and abandoned the people I was supposed to be protecting.

"There is nothing you can do for them," Procopius assured me when I voiced my guilt, "even if you had somehow defeated the Franks, you cannot fight famine. Whether by starvation or the blade, the people of Liguria and Tuscany are doomed to perish."

He was a hard-headed man, practically devoid of compassion, but I was forged of softer metal. Finally, when I could bear the shame no longer, and was haunted by the screams of dying Italians in my dreams, I gave the order to march out.

"I will do my duty," I said firmly, "and meet the Franks in the field, as I should have done weeks ago."

"Your duty is not to die," Procopius argued, but I refused to listen. Leaving him behind in Fiesole, I led out my six thousand men, with trumpets playing and banners flying, to seek the enemy.

What I found was a desert, littered with rotting corpses and the gaunt shades of the living. We encountered some Frankish soldiers a few miles north of Fiesole, though they could hardly be described as soldiers anymore: rather, a band of wandering ghouls with sunken eyes and swollen bellies, their minds gone, reduced to the most basic urges.

They took little notice of us, but fell like a pack of snarling dogs on some desiccated weeds growing by the roadside. One man managed to pull a fistful of weeds from the ground, and tried to make off with the booty, but was seized and dragged down by two of his comrades. They throttled him, and tore out his eyes, and turned on each other even as he jerked in his death-throes.

It seemed a kindness to kill them, and I ordered a troop of my horse-archers to shoot them down. When the Franks were dead, lying riddled with arrows, we marched on, leaving their corpses to bake and blacken in the pitiless heat.

I saw worse horrors, the further we advanced into Liguria, and the memories haunt me still. The Frankish host was disintegrating, murdered by the all-consuming famine. The remains of their broken, starving battalions strewn like so much human rubbish about the countryside.

The ghastly aspect of the dead was surpassed by the living, the little groups of survivors we encountered, their skin grey and lifeless and clinging to their bones. It was easy to identify those who had turned cannibal and survived by feasting on the flesh of former comrades. These men had a wild and fearful look, their hollow eyes shining with maniac fury, even as their hands swung listlessly by their sides.

We caught one such group of monsters in the act of devouring a corpse. They offered no resistance, but ran howling into the wilderness, their lips and fingers dripping with blood. Sickened, I ordered no pursuit, but had the half-eaten remnant of their comrade given a decent burial.

What was left of Theodobert's army crawled back across the Po and encamped on the northern bank. They devoured the last of their oxen, and drew water from the river, only to be hit by fresh disaster: the summer heat carried fever with it, and disease swept through the Frankish camp, carrying away a third of their number.

In this enfeebled state, the Franks were in no condition to refuse Belisarius' terms, which I delivered to King Theodobert in my capacity as envoy.

The Frankish camp stank of death. I rode through it with a cloth soaked in vinegar and fragrant spices pressed to my face. Emaciated, haggard-faced men were digging pits to bury their comrades. Neat rows of bodies covered in white sheets lay beside them, ready to be pushed in.

There were no horses. As Belisarius said, the Franks had little in the way of cavalry, and those beasts they did bring over the Alps had long since vanished down the throats of their starving warriors.

Theodobert received me in faded barbarian splendour. He sat before his tent in a high-backed wooden chair set on a bearskin rug. His surviving nobles and hearth-guards stood either side of the chair. Tall, well-made men, with long auburn beards and moustaches. I had last seen their like in Paris, when I fled there with my mother after Camlann.

I ran my eye over their armour and weapons, noting their long swords and double-edged axes, glittering mail, fine cloaks and elaborately decorated helms. I also noted the sullen, wasted look of the men under the gear, and the rank stench of sickness and death that hovered over all this martial display like a poisonous cloud.

The king was a youngish man, of medium height and slender build. His hair and beard were yellow, with a touch of grey, and he wore a slender golden circlet over a furrowed brow. Only the ice in his grey eyes hinted at the cruelty and ruthlessness that defined his character.

"Lord king," I said, bowing slightly, "I am Coel ap Amhar ap Arthur, envoy of General Belisarius. I bring you greetings from him, and a message."

Theodobert raked me with his eyes, and stretched out one yellow, claw-like hand.

"There is no letter, lord king. The general bade me repeat his message to you."

"Am I not worth a letter, then?" said Theodobert in a hoarse growl, "is the King of the Franks not worth the price of wax and parchment?"

I said nothing, not wishing to anger him. My escort consisted of a mere twenty lancers, and our lives rested in his hands.

He made an impatient gesture. "Repeat your master's words, then."

"General Belisarius advises you to put aside your ambitions of conquering Italy, or else risk the imperial displeasure. It would surely be wiser to maintain the tranquil and undisputed enjoyment of your hereditary lands, than to endanger their possession in the vain hope of extending their limits. Withdraw, then, back over the mountains into Frankia, and Belisarius will not hinder or pursue your retreat."

I spoke with some confidence, knowing the Franks were in dire straits. In other circumstances the fierce and treacherous Theodobert might have thrown the general's words back in my teeth, or had my head returned to him on a platter, but he dared not offer any insult now.

He didn't even consult with his nobles before responding. "I accept," he said, with all the grace and good humour of a man suffering from some terrible internal pain, "my people shall quit this hellish, Godforsaken land, and leave Belisarius and Vitiges to quarrel over its bones."

I gave silent thanks to God. The last major threat to the Roman cause in Italy had been repelled, and I could turn my thoughts to Ravenna.

And Arthur.

14.

The final march on Ravenna was preceded by the fall of Osimo, the last major Gothic stronghold in central Italy. Belisarius almost lost his life under the walls, when a sharp-eyed Gothic archer spotted him and loosed an arrow, but one of his bodyguards threw himself in front of the general. The arrow transfixed the guard's hand, which had to be amputated to save his life.

Enraged by the attempt on his life, and the loss of a good fighting man, Belisarius gave one of his rare displays of ruthlessness.

Osimo was well-supplied with water via an ancient cistern, and his engineers had been unable to destroy the solid architecture or divert the stream.

"If we cannot deprive the Goths of water, then let us taint it," he said, and gave orders for the corpses of dead soldiers to be thrown into the water supply, along with poisonous herbs and powdered lime.

Soon the Goths began to sicken and die. Terrified by the fate of their comrades, and the fury of Belisarius, the survivors quickly offered their surrender.

All our available forces were now concentrated on Ravenna. This city, the strongest in Italy, seemed to be impregnable. Surrounded by high walls, strong ramparts and impassable marshes, it had been chosen by Augustus as the principal station for the imperial fleet.

By this time the sea was slowly receding from the Italian peninsula, and the sandbanks near Classe (the harbour built by Augustus) were every day left dry and exposed by the ebbing of the tide. Procopius, who made detailed sketches of the city from a safe vantage point, also noted orchards growing near the harbour.

The city was still accessible by sea, and the Gothic fleet patrolled the Adriatic coastline to guard against any attempt at blockade.

"Well, Coel, what do you think of it?" asked Procopius when our army arrived before its walls, "Ravenna, home of the latter-day Western Emperors. A jewel of the West. Greater, perhaps, than Rome herself."

I ran my eye over the city's fearsome defences, the double line of walls and strong gates and high towers. Hundreds of steel helmets glinted along the extensive ramparts. Vitiges had withdrawn most of his army inside the walls, abandoning the rest of Italy to the Romans.

"I think," I replied, "that it will be a bastard of a place to take. There must be fifty or sixty thousand Goths in there, cooped up like rats, with their backs to the sea. Belisarius cannot hope to take the place by storm."

I squared my shoulders, and sighed. "That means another long siege. Perhaps the longest yet. We could sit outside Ravenna for years."

Narses finished his latest sketch, a map of the outer defences worked in charcoal on vellum, and inspected it critically before responding. "That's no good to you, is it? You need to get inside, as soon as possible, and find your son."

"If he exists," I said bluntly, "Narses may have lied to try and turn me against Belisarius."

"Who can say? Narses is a born liar, but occasionally speaks the truth to serve his own crooked ends."

He rose from his stool. "I have no intention of growing old here, waiting for Vitiges to surrender or be murdered by one of his generals. Nor, I suspect, does Belisarius."

Procopius knew the general's mind, better than any. Belisarius was indeed determined to crack open Ravenna's defences and bring the war to an end. He was still in secret correspondence with Matasontha, Vitiges' treacherous wife, though he did not use me as an envoy at this stage.

I cannot say what messages passed between them, but several days after the siege began Ravenna suddenly erupted with flame.

It was past midnight when the great fire started. The conflagration lit up the night sky and illuminated the countryside for miles around. Our soldiers, myself included, cheered the sight of Ravenna burning. Rumours flew through the camp of how it had been achieved.

"That is no accident," said Procopius, shivering in his night-gown, "see where the fire spreads, near the harbour? It's all granaries and storehouses there. Our agents are destroying their supplies."

There seemed little doubt the fire was started deliberately, and the frantic efforts of the Goths to douse the flames proved ineffectual. All night the city blazed, warming the hearts of our men, and the grey morning skies were partially obscured by clouds of blackish smoke drifting over the harbour.

Deprived of grain, Vitiges had no hope of withstanding a lengthy siege. Every soul in our army, down to the meanest pot-boy, knew and appreciated this, and a jubilant mood settled over the Roman camp. The last enemy outpost would soon be in our hands, and we could all go home – home at last, after almost two years of ceaseless warfare against a numerous and stubborn enemy.

I am not a particularly devout man, but I turned to my prayers like never before, begging the Almighty to spare my son. When the city fell, as fall it must, I feared our men would run wild, and Ravenna would go the same way as Naples and Milan: given over to an orgy of freebooting, rape and general destruction. Even Belisarius, generally a strict and effective disciplinarian, had no means of controlling his soldiers once a city fell to the sack.

Elene also featured in my prayers. "Let her be dead when I find her," I pleaded, "do not make me face her, lord. Forgive my sins, and spare me that."

Ideally, I would have liked to sink Caledfwlch into the traitress's heart, or hand her over to Belisarius for justice. Arthur, however, might hate me for bringing about the death of his mother. If he was indeed my son, I wanted his love. Only my long-dead mother had ever truly loved me, and I was sick of being alone in the world.

Vitiges had one last trick to play. Before we marched on Ravenna, he had despatched two of his nobles on a ship for Constantinople. There they prostrated themselves before Justinian and made a desperate series of threats and promises.

"Know, Caesar," they warned, "we have sent envoys to Nurshivan, dread King of the Sassanids, and he has agreed to invade Roman territory if you do not agree to peaceful terms with our master. To smooth the path to peace, King Vitiges offers to give up the southern part of Italy to your dominion, as well as the greater portion of his private treasury at Ravenna."

The Emperor should have laughed in their faces, but he feared the power of Nurshivan, poised just across our poorly-defended eastern borders with half a million warriors thirsting for battle. He also feared and envied Belisarius, though the general had never done anything but carry out his wishes, and suspected him of secretly desiring the Italian crown.

In spite of all the Roman blood and gold that had been spilled in Italy, Justinian agreed to a shameful treaty. Vitiges was to be left the title of King, a portion of his treasures, and all the provinces north of the Po. The rest of Italy, already won by the valour and skill of Belisarius, would once again be part of the Roman Empire.

The treaty was concluded without the knowledge of Belisarius, and with the connivance of Narses, who had never ceased to plot against his rival. The Gothic envoys sailed back to Ravenna with the glorious news for their sovereign, while a Roman ship carried an imperial ambassador to Belisarius, with orders for him to lift the siege.

I was not present when the ambassador laid the treaty before Belisarius, but Procopius was, and told me what passed.

"He sat rigid in his chair," the secretary later informed me, "and a shadow passed across his face. I have seen that shadow before, on the faces of dying men. For a moment I thought he had suffered a seizure. He did not move or speak until I ordered his guards to usher the ambassador out of the pavilion."

"What then?" I asked.

"He called for wine and started to drink. You know how he can drink when he sets his mind to it. Three flagons of sweet red nectar vanished down his gullet before he spoke again. He wildly cursed the Emperor, and the Empire, and the day he, Belisarius, had been born to serve the two-faced eagle of Rome. Then he fell off his chair, and I helped his attendants to get him into bed."

Belisarius did not emerge until late in the afternoon. Ashen-faced and trembling, he summoned a council of his senior officers to discuss the treaty.

Or, rather, to deny it. "The King of the Goths has offered to send Justinian a portion of his treasure," he said, "but I will carry Vitiges to Constantinople in chains, and present his person and all his treasure before the imperial throne. There will be no peace with the Goths except on my terms."

To my horror and astonishment, every one of his senior men betrayed him. None would agree to carry on the siege against the wishes of the Emperor, and each submitted in writing his reasons for accepting the proposed treaty. Even the likes of Bessas and Hildiger, the old war-horses, failed to support their chief.

"Traitors," he spat, "you, who have followed my banner and eaten my bread and taken my pay, now set me at nothing. To hell with you all. I am still commander-in-chief of Caesar's armies in Italy, and I say there will be no peace. Unless one of you wishes to challenge my authority?"

He stared at each men in turn, but none dared meet his gaze. Having cowed his officers, he packed the imperial ambassador back aboard his ship, and informed the Goths that the siege would continue.

Vitiges had learned to fear his enemy, and placed no faith in the treaty unless it came with the signature and oath of Belisarius. Naturally, the general refused to give either, and laid before the Goths a simple choice: surrender, or starve.

At the height of this bitter stalemate, I was ushered into the general's presence at dead of night, escorted by two of his Veterans.

Belisarius was alone inside his pavilion. A fire burned in a brazier on a tripod before his chair, and he was staring into the burning red coals, his pale hands folded on his lap.

"Coel," he murmured without looking up, "are you ready to do your duty?"

I saluted. "Always, sir."

"Good. You have never failed me. You, and Procopius. I rate your loyalty even higher than his."

I was nervous without the comforting presence of Procopius, who seemed to exert a calming influence on his master.

Belisarius picked up his sword, which lay unsheathed on the floor, and used it to poke the coals. "I am sick, Coel," he said wearily, "sick in mind and body."

I studied him carefully. He always looked ill, over-strained by work and responsibility, but I saw no sign of any serious malady.

"Rome has made me sick. All my life I have laboured in her service, toiling from one end of the Empire to another. Stamping out fires, shoring up our crumbling ramparts. But for me, Rome might have long since toppled into the abyss."

He spoke without a trace of arrogance. It was perfectly true. Without Belisarius, the eastern borders of the empire might have long since been overrun. It was he who drove back the Sassanids; who saved Justinian's throne by putting down the Nika riots; who destroyed the Vandal nation and re-conquered North Africa; who rolled back the tide of barbarians in Italy and defended the Eternal City against a colossal horde of Goths.

"You are owed much, sir," I ventured.

He lifted his left hand, as though he meant to scratch his cheek, and then lowered it. "Yes. Owed much. Few men get what they are owed in this life. They get what they earn. What they take."

His hand came up again, and curled into a fist. "Come here," he ordered.

I stepped closer to his chair. "I said I would use you as an envoy," he said, "and now your time has come. You will carry no more precious message than this. Again, as when I despatched you to the camp of Theodobert, there will be nothing in writing. Listen, and take note."

"Thanks to the recent fire in Ravenna, deliberately started by the servants of Queen Matasontha, the Goths are starving. They begged me to accept the Emperor's treaty, but I refused. Nothing will induce me to accept it. I will never betray the memory of my soldiers. Not the officers, that pack of treacherous ingrates, but the rank and file, who have fought and died for me and left their bones in Italian soil."

He slowly turned his head and looked directly at me. "Not for Rome," he said with emphasis, "but me. Their general."

He suddenly changed tack. "Do you remember what I said to you, Coel? That your homeland might yet be saved?"

"Yes, sir," I replied, startled by the question, "I remember it well."

"I meant every word. For months now, I have been considering the future. Where has all my loyalty, all my sacrifice, brought me? To the edge of ruin. The Emperor doesn't trust me. He hates and envies me, and sends his disgusting favourites to undermine my efforts on his behalf."

He leaned forward in his chair and stared deeper into the spitting coals. "God has made my decision for me. Two nights ago I received a messenger from inside Ravenna. Not from Matasontha, but Vitiges. He has agreed to abdicate and surrender his capital to me."

My jaw dropped at this wonderful news, but Belisarius was not done.

"Mark that, Coel. They have surrendered, not to Rome, but to me."

"Sir," I said, "you are Rome. Rome's greatest living general."

"No. Not any longer. I am done with Rome, as she is done with me. Vitiges and his council have agreed to surrender Ravenna, and the whole of Italy, on one condition."

His eyes bored into mine. "They have offered me the crown of Italy, and to resurrect the title of Western Emperor. I will be crowned in Ravenna as King of the Goths and Emperor of the West."

"Think of it, Coel. I have spent all my career fighting barbarians. Now I shall unite all the barbarian tribes of the West under my banner. Combined with my army and fleet, we shall be unstoppable. I shall march on Constantinople, hurl Justinian and his whore of a wife from the thrones they have disgraced for so long, and purge the court of vipers like

Narses and John the Sanguinary. That done, the crowns of East and West shall be united in my person, and the scattered fragments of the Roman Empire re-forged anew."

I tried to speak, to think. Seized by this incredible new vision, I failed miserably at both.

"You, Coel, are destined to rise higher yet in my favour. I can think of no-one better. When the time is right, and the lost provinces of Frankia and Germania are once again under the sway of Rome, I shall send you to your native land with Caesar's sword at your hip, and Caesar's armies at your back. Coel ap Amhar ap Arthur, my *magister militum*. You shall cross the sea to the island of Britain, drive out the Saxon pirates that infest it, and bring her back into the imperial fold!"

15.

I was sent into Ravenna under a flag of truce, and with a sizeable escort of Belisarius' Veterans. Officially, I entered the city to negotiate Justinian's proposed treaty. Unofficially, I was to inform Vitiges and his council that Belisarius accepted their offer, and was happy to betray his imperial master for the Italian crown and title of Western Emperor.

We were met by a Gothic officer and a retinue of lancers, and led to the royal palace, where Vitiges had his headquarters.

The palace was built by Theoderic the Great, the best of the Gothic monarchs. It made me ashamed to think of him as a barbarian. Built on the site of an old Roman palace, it was built of white stone and marble and colonnaded in the old style, a residence fit for Augustus himself.

"A fine place, eh?" said the officer, smiling at me, "or perhaps you expected to find the King of the Goths living in a timber hut, with smoke escaping from a hole in the thatch?"

He was young for his rank, tall and slender and red-haired, with no beard on his chin. I was amused by his conceit. The Goths had long since adopted the manners and customs of civilised folk, and come a long way from their brutish ancestors, who used to live in draughty wooden halls and gnaw their meat with bloody fingers.

I struggled my maintain my outwardly calm appearance, suitable for an envoy of Rome, as I entered the vast, echoing halls of the palace, and trod the beautifully inlaid mosaics decorating the floors of Theoderic's home. I had seen palatial splendour before. Nothing here rivalled the magnificence of the Great Palace in Constantinople.

My mind and soul were elsewhere. Belisarius had lit new fires inside me. His vision of a new Roman Empire, forged from the shattered remains of the old, was both overwhelming and irresistible.

It was also no idle daydream. Belisarius was a hero to his troops, if not the officers, and they would happily follow him to the gates of Hell. Far lesser Roman generals had won the love of their soldiers, and led successful rebellions against corrupt and incompetent emperors.

It was rank treason, of course. All our necks would be forfeit if the attempt failed. Justinian would show no mercy. For my part, I had no cause to love the Emperor. He had deliberately kept the army starved of adequate supplies and reinforcements, and plainly cared nothing for the lives of the soldiers he used to gratify his own insatiable pride and ambition.

Nor did I fear him. He was no soldier himself, and none of his loyal generals were a match for Belisarius. When our united host marched on Constantinople, Justinian would most likely flee into exile, or throw himself on the mercy of his former servant.

I thrilled to the prospect of seeing his foul wife, the Empress Theodora, loaded down with chains and paraded along the Mese before jeering crowds. She had once murdered a friend of mine, and done her best to serve me the same way. I hated her more than Narses and Antonina and all the rest of my enemies put together.

The officer's voice broke in on my thoughts. "I said, you don't have the look of an Easterner," he said.

"My apologies," I muttered, "I'm not from the East. I am a Briton in the service of Rome."

We had reached a large antechamber with a vaulted roof. A huge pair of iron doors, three times my height and inscribed with scenes of hunting and battle, stood closed before us. Two hard-faced Gothic spearmen in green cloaks and twinkling mail flanked the doors.

"A Briton," he said, "that is unusual these days. Britain has been independent from Rome for over a century."

I didn't like his questioning tone, or the intense way he stared at me. "My origins are none of your concern," I snapped, "I came here to speak to King Vitiges, not engage in idle chat with his underlings."

He murmured an apology, and said nothing more until the doors swung inward, dragged open by a troop of slaves.

The doors opened onto the throne room, a rectangular hall with a high ceiling and a central avenue lined with rows of black marble pillars. A guardsman stood before each pillar, armed with spear and shield. The avenue was decorated with another gorgeous mosaic, this one depicting a king abasing himself before Christ, and ended in a short flight of marble steps.

The steps led to a dais, upon which King Vitiges sat on his throne. He sat with his chin resting on his fist, and didn't move a muscle as the officer led me towards him.

Vitiges' consort, Matasontha, sat beside her husband on a noticeably smaller throne. They made a handsome couple, still young, with the corn-gold hair and blue eyes of their folk. Vitiges was stocky and bow-legged, somewhat shorter than his wife.

Both were dressed in royal splendour. Their brows were adorned with slender royal circlets, and they wore loose mantles of purple silk, lined with gold and fastened at the shoulder with elaborate golden brooches. Vitiges wore a belt made of silver and gold links, carved in the shapes of stags and wild boar. His sword, a broad-bladed weapon with a short blade, hung from his hip in a wool-lined sheath.

There was a terrible sadness in the king's eyes as he silently watched us approach the throne. This was his last act as King of the Goths, and he knew it.

I halted at a respectful distance and bowed before him. "Your Majesty," I said formally, "General Belisarius sends his greetings."

Vitiges shifted slightly. At close quarters, he looked older than I first thought. There was a grey pallor to his roughly handsome features, and a general air of dejection about him. He spoke with none of the royal hauteur and arrogance I expected, but like a man who knew his time was up.

"Has he," he began, before swallowing, closing his eyes and trying again, "has he accepted our terms?"

"He has, majesty. The crown of Italy, the title of Western Emperor, and the fealty of your soldiers. In return, you will be allowed to go free, and depart from Italy after swearing an oath on holy relics never to set foot in the kingdom again."

He nodded, and glanced at his wife. "What of my queen?"

I turned to face Matasontha, and the breath caught in my throat. She was a rare beauty, if somewhat faded, and like Theodora relied on the artifice of cosmetics to sustain her fair looks.

Matasontha was also Theodora's equal in treachery, though doubtless she would claim all was done for the good of her nation. There was some justice in that. Her husband's stubborn insistence on fighting the Romans, even after so many defeats and terrible losses, had brought little good to their people.

"Matasontha will retain a portion of her treasure, and also be permitted to go free," I said, trying not to wilt under the lash of her deep blue eyes, "but will relinquish the title of Queen of the Goths. As King-Emperor of the West, Belisarius will have no other consort but his own wife, Antonina."

Whether Matasontha had expected more, I cannot be certain, but she suffered the loss of her royal status in dignified silence.

Vitiges reached across to lay a comforting hand on his wife's arm. She sat rigid, like a statue, and failed to acknowledge his touch.

"So be it," he sighed, "tomorrow morning, Ravenna will open her gates, and Belisarius may occupy the city. I will receive him here, in this chamber, and hand over my crown."

I bowed again. "There is something more," I said after a pause, "Belisarius regards me as a trusted servant, and has granted me a favour. He insists that you fulfil it."

This was true. I had demanded it of the general, as the price for my betrayal of Justinian.

"Name it," said Vitiges, looking wary.

"There is a woman named Elene in your household. A Greek, just recently arrived in Ravenna. She has a son named Arthur."

For the first time, Matasontha showed signs of life. She lifted her proud head and moved her arm away from Vitiges' hand. Elene was clearly not a name she wanted to hear.

"I want Arthur," I said forcefully, "you will hand him over to my care and custody. As for Elene, I have no interest in her. She is to leave Ravenna. Tonight. Now. I care not where she goes, but her son stays with me."

"You have an interest in the lad?" asked Vitiges, momentarily distracted from his own troubles.

"Yes. I am his father."

According to Procopius, Elene had served Vitiges as one of his whores. If he loved her, he concealed it well, and made no effort to protect her.

"Granted," he said, looking sadly at his wife. Matasontha was staring straight ahead, over my shoulder. I suspect Procopius was correct. The king's repeated infidelities had affronted her proud spirit, and caused her to betray him to his enemies.

I was courteously ushered out of the throne room, and given supper in a smaller room leading off the antechamber. Meanwhile Vitiges despatched the young officer and six of his royal guards to find Elene and Arthur.

"They are still lodged in the palace," he explained, "near my own quarters. Eat and drink your fill, and be comfortable. My men shall soon return."

Unable to eat, I pushed away the platter of salt beef and sat trembling with fear and nervous excitement. I was going to see my son. After all these years, we would clap eyes on each other for the first time.

Endless questions swirled through my mind. How would he react to me? Would he rush into my arms, or spring at me with a curse on his lips? He must have something of his mother in him. I prayed he had not inherited her gift for hating.

Time crawled past. After an age, the young Gothic officer appeared in the doorway.

Like me, he trembled, and tears coursed down his beardless cheeks. I half-rose, and instinctively reached for Caledfwlch.

"You won't need that," he said, his voice full of misery and despair, "Elene is dead. She took her own life rather than spend it without me. Are you content now, father?"

16.

Elene lay in her bath, the blood from her slit wrists gently expanding to turn the water a cloudy red.

She looked peaceful in death, almost serene. The years had left little mark on her, save a few grey hairs in her long, glossy black hair, now unbound and dabbled in blood.

Orphaned as a baby, Elene had been raised in the Hippodrome and trained as a dancer. Her body was as lean and wiry and muscular as ever. I remembered the warmth of it, coiled around me in bed during the distant days of our shared youth.

The warmth and life was gone from her forever. Her dancer's body was naught but a lifeless piece of meat, floating in dirty water. Her shade had fled, hopefully to some peaceful haven.

The moment I heard she was dead, all my hatred for Elene dissipated like morning mist.

I tore my eyes away from the terrible, pitiful sight, to face her son. Our son.

We were alone in his mother's quarters. Arthur had dismissed the rest of the guard, and brought me here by himself. I thought he meant to kill me.

"Here," I said, loosening Caledfwlch in her scabbard and offering him the hilt, "if you're going to do it, use your great-grandsire's blade. I won't try and stop you."

His face was still streaked with tears. At just sixteen, he was already a head taller than me, and would grow to be a giant. He had his mother's wiry frame, of the sort that does not carry fat, and the red hair and fair colouring of his royal British ancestors. My heart swelled with grief and pride to look at him. The grief was for myself; the pride all for him. It was obvious, just by his appearance, that my grandsire's blood ran far stronger in his veins than mine.

He had his mother's eyes, large and green and fiercely expressive. They fastened on Caledfwlch.

"Caesar's sword," he murmured, wiping his face with the back of his gauntlet, "I have heard so much about it. The twin Roman eagles, stamped in gold on an ivory hilt."

"Your inheritance," I said, "take it now, if you like."

Arthur's gaze lingered my sword for a moment. Then he drew himself up, towering above me, and patted the hilt of the spatha hanging from his hip. "I have my own sword," he replied sternly, "and have no interest in old heirlooms."

"When you saw my mother, lying dead in the water," he asked, "what did you feel? Shame? Guilt? Or nothing at all?"

He rapped out the questions like an officer used to command. The harsh, soldierly tone concealed the undoubted pain ravaging his soul.

"Sadness," I answered truthfully, "but no shame or guilt. Elene chose to leave me, all those years ago. She chose to betray me, to lie to me, to try and have me killed. She betrayed her employers, and the Empire, and eventually ran out of places to hide."

I shook my head, trying not to look at the thing in the bath. "You knew her better than I, but it seems to me Elene tried to use treachery as a weapon. Unlike others, she lacked the skill to wield it."

Arthur's index finger tap-tapped on the hilt of his sword. I watched it closely, waiting for him to draw steel. I was testing him, seeing how far he could be pushed, trying to divine his feelings for Elene.

"She never betrayed me," he said quietly, "for years we led a vagabond life, wandering Anatolia and Syria, begging for our keep most of the time. We often had little to eat, but that little always went to me first. My earliest memory is of her weeping with hunger as she pushed bread into my mouth."

It was too much. I lifted my hand in a silent plea for mercy.

"Why?" I burst out when I could trust myself to speak again, "why did she leave me? There was no need for such hardship – no need to expose herself, and you, to such suffering! I would have provided for both of you."

To my astonishment, Arthur laughed. It was the bitterest laugh I ever heard, full of contempt and mockery, and the last thing I expected to hear. His mother's body lay cooling in the bath, just a few feet away, with a bloody knife lying on the flagstones beside the stone tub, and yet he laughed.

"She didn't want you!" he cried, "she didn't want to be any man's wife, looking after his hearth and home, preparing his meals, submitting to his desires in bed. My mother was a lone wolf, angry and frustrated with the limits placed on her sex. She should have been born a man. What a soldier she would have made!"

He looked at me pityingly. "She didn't love you. She loved nothing and no-one, save me."

Suddenly I was angry. "Very well, she didn't love me," I retorted, "but I did nothing to incur her hatred. Why did she try to have me killed outside Naples?"

Arthur hung his head, and ran a hand through his thick mop of red curls.

"I don't know, for certain. I suspect she held a grudge against you for putting a child in her belly. Nature compelled her to love me, so she turned all her anger and resentment on you. No-one could hate like Elene. When I was eight years old, she turned her hand to killing for money. An assassin, hiring out her services to the highest bidder. Turned out she had a rare talent for it. A passion for dealing death. We lived well, until she took service with Antonina, and failed her once too often."

"And you?" I asked, "did she teach you to hate?"

"I was always a disappointment to her in that regard. She tried to turn me into a killer, to teach me the ways of the assassin. No-one suspects a child, do they? I could slip poison into a man's drink, or a subtle knife into his back, and escape before anyone noticed I had gone. I refused to do it. Why should I? I had no cause to hate anyone."

"Still, she kept me by her side through the years. As I grew, I became her protector, her shield against the buffets of the world."

He eyed me with a cynical smile on his lips, far too cynical for one so young. "I suspected who you were, as soon as you told me you were British. Your continued survival drove her mad. In the end, she decided you were not quite mortal, and that she was fated to die by your hand."

"But she died by her own," I said heavily.

"Yes. She preferred death by the knife, in the warm and comfort of her bath, than the humiliation of being defeated by you. Disgraced Roman senators used to open their veins in the bath. I believe she was following their example, and tried to make a noble end."

"I was ready to kill you in the throne room," he added, "even though I knew you were my father. If you had asked Vitiges to put Elene to death, I was going to draw my sword and run you through the heart. Vitiges would have executed me, of course, but I cared little for my own life. I could not see my mother end on the gallows, or by the headsman's blade."

In the end, I left him to grieve. It was unbearable, being in the presence of such a miserable death, and I could feel the weight of all Elene's wasted years pressing down on me.

Somehow, though I claimed to feel no guilt, the blame was mine. For whatever reason, I had not been good enough for her, and the result of my inadequacy lay bleeding in a lukewarm bath.

For the present, I had exhausted all I had to say to Arthur. He had shocked me, and frightened me a little, and finally left me baffled. His love and sorrow for Elene was evident, but there was something unknowable about him. In time, when his grief had passed and Elene was safely in the ground, I hoped to become his friend.

I was obliged to leave Ravenna the same evening, to inform Belisarius of the success of my mission. He was elated, the happiest I had seen him in many a year, and warmly congratulated me on finding my son.

"God has not seen fit to bless me in that regard, alas," he said, shaking my hand (he had just one child, a daughter from a previous marriage), "but I wish you joy of him. Arthur, is his name? Ha, your grandsire lives again!"

I had come to a similar conclusion. Later, in the peace and solitude of my tent, I permitted myself the luxury of grand dreams.

Thanks to the discovery of Arthur, my chaotic, rootless existence now made sense. All had become clear. Belisarius would assume control of the restored Roman Empire and despatch me, at the head of an army, to make Britain a Roman province once again.

The stories of my grandsire insisted that he had not died at Camlann, but had been spirited away to Avallon, the legendary Isle of Apples, to recover from his wounds in a deathless sleep. When the time came, and Britain was in deadly peril, he would awake and return at the head of his warriors to save the country.

My mind raced with possibilities. The prophecy of my grandsire's return would be fulfilled in the person of my son, another Arthur. He would return to Britain, with me at his side, and drive out the barbarians who had plagued the land for generations.

It was not I who would sit in royal state, with the glittering crown of the High King of Britain on my brow, and Caledfwlch at my hip. That glorious destiny was reserved for my son. My task was to bring it about.

My dreams that night were full of kings and crowns, dim battles fought beside a misted shore, the cries of dying men, the dying blast of war-horns, and the harsh croak of ravens as they feasted on the slain.

My youth had been haunted by such dreams, but I had not experienced any for years, ever since I slew the traitor Leo in the Hippodrome. I welcomed their return, and gloried in the vivid, bloodstained imagery of war. They were glimpses, I assured myself, of the glorious victories Arthur would win over the pagans in Britain.

Not once, in my fevered imaginings, did I consider the wishes of my son. He, like me, was inextricably bound up in the coils of fate. There was no escaping his destiny. Why should he wish to?

The night passed, dreams faded, and the sound of trumpets pierced the morning air, announcing the surrender of Ravenna.

17.

On a cold, bright dawn in mid-December, the gates of the Gothic capital were thrown open, and Belisarius led his army in triumph through the streets. His fleet, laden with provisions to sweeten the mood of the starving populace, was permitted to sail into the harbour at Classe.

The sailors immediately started distributing bread and wine to the citizens. Belisarius well understood how to win the affection of the mob, and that the fame and terror of his name were sometimes not enough to guarantee it.

I rode in the vanguard, among his Veterans, wearing the fine armour he had given me at Fermo. The imperial banner flew in triumph above my head, and thousands of people lined the streets to look upon their deliverer – or conqueror, depending on how you look at it – General Flavius Belisarius, the most famous soldier of the age.

"Shame!" I overheard some of the Gothic women cry, "shame!"

I thought their shouts were directed at me, but then I saw them spitting in the faces of their menfolk and pointing in derision at our troops.

They were heaping shame on their husbands and brothers and sons, the men of the Gothic nation, for being conquered by the Romans, whom they regarded as degenerate and effeminate. Certainly, most of our soldiers lacked the physical size and strength of the Goths. To the women, who knew little of war, it must have seemed impossible that a vastly outnumbered army of pygmy hirelings could have overcome their warriors in so many battles.

Belisarius was careful to restrain his men from looting the city, not wishing to spoil the glory of this, his final and decisive victory. Having surrendered peacefully, Ravenna was spared the horrors of the sack, and Belisarius's accession to the throne of Italy untainted by the blood of innocents.

First, he had to formally claim the crown from Vitiges. Clad in his golden ceremonial armour, he dismounted before the steps of the palace, and entered on foot with two hundred Veterans marching at his back. The imperial banner was put aside, and trumpeters and drummers announced his arrival, filling the halls of Theoderic's palace with triumphant noise.

I marched in the front rank of Veterans, between Bessas and Hildiger. Procopius hurried to keep step beside us, carrying a folded robe of purple and gold silk. Imperial robes, destined to be draped over his master's shoulders at the height of the crowning ceremony.

We expected no resistance, and encountered none. Vitiges had ordered his guards to lay down their arms. The proudest of them had refused, and languished in chains under the palace, but the rest knelt in submission as we marched past. No longer soldiers of an independent Gothic kingdom, but subjects of Belisarius, King-Emperor of the West.

Vitiges and his chief councillors were waiting for us in the throne room. The ex-King of the Goths, now dressed in a plain blue mantle and tunic, stood at the foot of the steps leading to the vacant throne. Queen Matasontha had already left him, departing from Ravenna in a cloud of dust and disapproval. A few loyal attendants had gone with her, along with several ox-drawn wagons containing her share of the royal treasure.

Four trembling old councillors, dressed in plain robes, knelt in the middle of the avenue leading to the throne. Between them they held a purple cushion. On the cushion gleamed the crown of Italy. A slender silver diadem, studded with flashing gemstones.

Without even glancing at the crown, Belisarius swept past the old men. Vitiges knelt in submission, but the general ignored him also, and mounted the steps of the dais.

The trumpets rang out once more, and his Veterans crashed to a halt. Belisarius turned to face us. A proud, imposing figure, tall and soldierly and dignified. Born to wear the purple.

I pictured Justinian, sitting in the heart of the Great Palace in Constantinople. Soon enough he would hear of his general's betrayal, and soil himself in terror.

Belisarius beckoned to Procopius, who climbed the steps of the dais and stood beside him.

"Bring forth the crown," he ordered, his voice full of confidence and authority. This was the true voice of Caesar.

The aged councillors struggled to their feet and advanced slowly across the mosaic. Their rheumy eyes were full of fear. Vitiges shuffled aside on his knees to make space for them. He was a sorry sight, utterly cowed and defeated, forced to watch his enemy take the crown he had failed to defend.

One of the old men, the least decrepit, reverently lifted the crown from its cushion and limped up the steps. Wincing at the cracking in his bony knees, he abased himself before Belisarius and offered up the crown.

Belisarius looked at it for the first time. An expectant silence hung over the chamber. He slowly stretched out his right hand and held it hovering over the precious diadem.

The hand curled into a fist.

"Soldiers," he cried, "arrest these men, in the name of Rome and the Emperor Justinian."

18.

The shadows lengthen in my cell. Winter has come. Her bony fingers creep through the thick walls of our abbey, touching the hearts of those who lack the strength to withstand her.

I am one of them. This shall be my last winter on earth, for which I thank God in His mercy. My spirit is ready to fly, to break free of this crumbling stronghold of flesh and bone, and look for its salvation.

Or damnation, if the Lord wills. I have done enough good and evil in my life to warrant either. Strange to think that, left to myself, I would have happily lived out my days in peaceful obscurity. For fifty years I was used by others before finding a degree of repose here, in this quiet abbey.

The abbot, Gildas, disapproves of my writings. "A Christian monk should spend his time in prayer and contemplation," he is fond of saying, "not recording the sins and sorrows of his past."

My answer is always the same. "What of your own histories, lord?" I ask in the mock-humble tone I know irritates him.

"They are sermons, Coel, not histories," he huffs, "intended to condemn the kings of Britain for their sins, and warn future generations to heed the word of the Lord."

We spend much of our remaining time like this, two old men, sitting in a freezing cell and arguing. It is one way to stay warm.

Gildas is famed for his learning and acerbic writing style. He keeps an extensive library – his only luxury – and is known to some as Gildas the Wise. His major work, *On the Ruin and Conquest of Britain,* describes events in Britain from the arrival of the legions to our own time.

It is a history, whatever he might claim, though shamelessly inaccurate and larded with the righteous fury of a holy man who thinks his people have abandoned God.

His chronicle makes no mention of my grandsire, the man who united the Britons, at least for a time, and held the land safe against barbarian conquest for twenty-one years. I have begged and pleaded with Gildas to relent, but he will have none of it.

"Arthur was a tyrant," he says firmly, "an uncrowned king who ruled by mere force of arms, and without legitimate authority. I care not how many battles he won against the heathen. He shall play no part in my narrative. I draw a veil over him."

I know the true reasons for Gildas' silence. Arthur executed a number of his kinsmen, British princes who rebelled against Arthur's authority and (God grant the abbot never reads this) forged treacherous alliances with the Saxons.

Treachery. It has been the constant theme of my life. Of all the betrayals and disappointments, the one that hurt me most, and defined the remainder of my life, was the one committed by Belisarius in the throne room of Theoderic's palace in Ravenna.

To do him credit, he made some effort to explain his actions to me, on the eve of his departure for Constantinople. Justinian had recalled him, not in disgrace – even he could not deny Belisarius' achievements in Italy – but not in triumph either. The general's enemies at court, headed by Narses, ensured Justinian's gratitude was forever poisoned by envy and suspicion.

"I am sorry," were his first words to me, when he summoned me to his quarters in the palace, "sorry for deceiving you. It was necessary. You must understand."

We were in the old royal chambers, once the private residence of Vitiges and his queen. In common with the rest of the palace, the floors were decorated with startling mosaics of many hues and complex designs, the walls pillared and colonnaded in white marble.

The ex-King of the Goths was now an honoured captive, destined to be taken back to Constantinople aboard Belisarius' flagship. Like Gelimer before him, he would be paraded along the Mese in chains before the cheering populace as the latest trophy of war. His ultimate fate would be decided by

Justinian, who had done little to defeat the brave Gothic king, and much to undermine the efforts of his own troops.

"Why?" I asked simply, "why was it necessary?"

Belisarius had the grace to look uncomfortable. "I needed to persuade Vitiges that I really intended to betray the Emperor. It was the only way of securing Ravenna without a siege. There was no better of making him believe the lie than sending an envoy who also believed it."

"Unworthy of me, I know," he said helplessly, "I daresay you expected better of your general. But it was a legitimate ruse of war. Consider, Coel. The city freely opened its gates to us, and not one Roman soldier died. Italy is restored to the Empire. We have achieved everything we set out to do here."

"At the price of your honour," I pointed out.

The scene of chaos in the throne room, after Belisarius had ordered his Veterans to arrest the Gothic councillors, was still vivid in my mind.

It was all pre-planned. Bessas and Hildiger rushed forward before I knew what was happening. The old men were seized, bleating feebly in protest. Vitiges tried to make a fight of it, but he was unarmed, and two of our Huns cracked his head against a pillar. He slumped to the ground, bleeding from his mouth and nostrils, and was quickly trussed up and dragged away.

Belisarius plucked the crown of Italy from its cushion between finger and thumb, and held it at arm's length.

"This degraded object," he said contemptuously, "shall adorn no more ambitious heads. Take it away."

He tossed it to his soldiers, who laughed and threw it about among themselves. Finally a grinning officer seized it and tucked it into his belt, to the good-natured groans of his men.

"My honour?" said Belisarius, back in the present, "what is that worth, compared to the glory of Rome? Those fools in Ravenna thought I was prepared to betray Caesar. They will have ample leisure to reflect on their mistake.

"So did I, sir," I reminded him, "time and again you promoted me, above my ability, and made a false promise regarding my homeland. You told me the Western Empire would be restored under your stewardship. That I would return to Britain at the head of an army, to drive out the barbarians threatening to destroy it. You made me dream impossible dreams, all for the sake of your ambition."

"No," he replied sternly, wagging a finger, "for the sake of Rome. Yes, I lied to you. I apologise. But you deserved the promotions. I have no more loyal and capable officer in my service."

"Had. I intend to resign my commission and retire from the army. Immediately."

His eyes widened. "Do nothing in haste, Coel. Your career…"

"I care nothing for my career. I am sick of it all. The army. The constant intrigues and betrayals. I want no more part of it."

Belisarius tried to persuade me otherwise, to assure me of my continued worth to him, but I stood firm. The treachery of Ravenna had broken something inside me. To be promised so much, and then have it snatched away and revealed as mere illusion, a trick to fool barbarians, was more than my pride could bear.

"I would remind you," he said when all his arguments were exhausted, "that a soldier of Rome is required to serve for a minimum of twenty-five years. You are nowhere near completing your term. The penalty for desertion is death."

I faced him calmly. "Then you will have to put me on trial, sir. I will not remain a moment longer in your service. In any case, I am not a young man, and Rome has had the best of me."

He was right, of course. I didn't have the option of voluntary retirement, but counted on him feeling that he owed me something. I had spilled enough of my blood on his behalf, in North Africa and Sicily and Italy, and he would gain little from forcing me to stay on.

"Very well," he said at last, "if you are determined on this course, I shall not hinder you. There will be no trial. But you will lose my friendship."

I said nothing, and I could see my silence wounded him. He could count the number of officers whose loyalty to him was absolute on the fingers of one hand. Their number had just diminished.

19.

I waited until the fleet had departed for
Constantinople, laden with prisoners and
plunder from the long campaign, and then
hired a small private ship to take me home.

Me, and my son. Arthur had buried his
mother in a private ceremony – I was invited,
but had no wish to go – and was at a loss. He
owed allegiance to no-one, having merely
posed as a Gothic officer, and had no wish to
serve in the garrison Belisarius left behind to
guard Ravenna.

I found him sitting on an upturned barrel on
a jetty, watching the last of our ships depart.
He had kept his armour and sword, and I felt
such a pang as I looked at him. Elene was
dead, but I could not forgive her for cheating
me of him. Of all those lost years, when I
might have loved and raised him as my own,
like a normal father.

"Come with me," I said, "to Constantinople.
There is nothing to keep either of us here."

A gentle breeze ruffled his hair as he gazed
out to sea. "I have seen the imperial city," he
murmured, "from afar. Mother always refused
to go back there."

"For good reason. We can both prosper
there. I have lost the favour of Belisarius, but
do not lack for money."

This was true. My friend Procopius had looked after my interests during the campaign, and taken care to set aside my share of the plunder from all the cities and fortresses our army had sacked. Along with my back pay, and the sale of the fine horse and armour Belisarius had presented me with at Fermo, I was, if not rich, at least comfortable.

Arthur smiled. He was a handsome boy, my superior in every respect.

"Mother wanted me to kill you," he said, "she never uttered your name without cursing it. And now here you are, offering me a chance of a new life. What would we do, go into business together?"

I nodded. "That is exactly what I have in mind. I am getting too old for the army, and have no wish to see you waste your life following the eagle, as I have. Come home with me, and let us spend my money wisely."

So we did. A fair wind blew us across the calm seas of the Adriatic, and barely two weeks later our ship was gliding up the Straits of Magellan. It was the easiest voyage I ever knew, even though Arthur, like me, was a martyr to sea-sickness. Between bouts of vomiting and praying for death, we came to know each other a little better.

I had never really confided in anyone before, save Procopius, and I had always been careful to feed him carefully selected bits of information. Procopius was a friend, but also a clever and self-interested man, and his first instinct was to use people to his advantage.

Arthur knew nothing of his family on my side. I had told Elene a fair deal, in the days when we were lovers, but she chose to keep her son in ignorance of his distinguished British ancestry.

He devoured the tales of his namesake, my grandsire, and of the glorious line of ancient British princes we were descended from.

"This sword," I said, running my hand along the gleaming blade of Caledfwlch, "has dropped in and out of our family's history. Nennius took it from Caesar, and then the enchanter Merlin gave it to Arthur. My mother gave Caledfwlch to me, and so, when the time comes, it shall pass to you."

I weighed the sword carefully in my hands. "It has always been the most precious thing in my life. I went to the far ends of the earth to retrieve it from the King of the Vandals. I believe the soul of Arthur resides inside the steel."

On impulse, I held it out to him. "Take it."

Arthur gaped at me, and at Caledfwlch. His face was pale and washed-out from sickness. "No," he said weakly, "I can't take it now. When you are gone, maybe…"

"Now," I said firmly, "I was never fit to wield Caledfwlch. You are Arthur's true heir."

He required some persuasion, but eventually consented to take the sword. I could sense he wanted it for himself, and was anxious to avoid causing any jealousy or resentment by making him wait for his birthright.

In truth, I was weary of the responsibility. Caesar's sword was a heavy burden, and I had always felt like a mere guardian rather than its owner. A stopgap, until a better man came along. Now he had, in the person of my son.

Arthur reverently took Caledfwlch. The pale morning sun caught the polished steel. For the second time in my life I saw Caesar's sword burst into silvery flame, a nimbus of light that rippled up the length of the blade and surrounded it in a kind of unearthly glow.

"The Flame of the West," I muttered. Caesar's sword bore many names, and now it had another.

The moment was spoiled somewhat when another spasm gripped Arthur's belly, and he was obliged to turn away to dry-heave over the side. I hoped it wasn't a bad omen, and patted him on the back until he had finished retching.

You may think me a fool for returning to Constantinople, where I had made so many powerful enemies. Perhaps I was foolish, but I was also sick of running, and living in fear of the glut of degenerates who governed the Empire.

There is a deep core of stubbornness to my character, and I had rejected my old notion of fleeing, beyond the borders of Rome. I gambled on being no threat to the likes of Antonina and Narses now, and of no interest either. Merely an ageing ex-soldier, looking to live out his declining years in peace. Besides, Constantinople had been my home since childhood, and I wanted to see it again, the jewel of the civilised world.

A plan was forming in my mind. By the time the walls and towers of Constantinople came in sight, and our little ship was rowing carefully around the edge of the great fleet nestling in the harbour of the Golden Horn, it was complete.

I would use my money to set up as a horse-dealer, one of the most profitable trades I knew, and supply beasts to the army and the merchant caravans that frequently passed through Constantinople. Not the most honourable trade for the descendent of princes, perhaps, but I was done with honour. It was a foolish conceit invented by those who knew nothing of the world, and the true character of mankind.

Done with honour, and war, and politics. The whole messy, bloody business.

For a time, God granted me the peace I craved. But nothing in life is permanent, and no man can elude his destiny.

20.

I remained in Constantinople for ten years, with Arthur at my side. My money from the Italian campaign purchased a fine set of stables on the Asiatic side of the city suburbs, including training grounds and a paddock.

As an ex-cavalry officer, I knew something of horses, and bought decent stock from stud farms in Hispania and North Africa. I bred and raised foals for the chariot races in the Hippodrome, for merchant caravans, and for the army, which had an inexhaustible need for cavalry mounts.

These were good years, perhaps the best of my life. As I hoped, my enemies no longer had any interest in me, and were too embroiled in their own affairs to waste time persecuting nonentities. I heard of the various court scandals and intrigues from afar, and thanked God I was no longer dragged into them.

I forged a successful working partnership with my son. At first he was wary of me, which was only natural, considering the lies Elene had fed him about his father. I took various measures to win his trust, including giving him a share in the business, a degree of responsibility, and a stipend to live on.

Perhaps I was too generous, and left myself open to being exploited, but Arthur never looked to take advantage. He was an easy-natured youth, quiet and hard-working, and never complained or demanded more than I gave him.

I never really got to know him. Even when we were alone together, sharing a last cup of wine after dinner before retiring, I was conscious of a certain reserve. Maybe it was due to his strange upbringing, wandering from place to place, always among strangers, always wondering where the next meal would come from, but he never revealed his inner soul. The gates to his true self were firmly locked and barred. I could only hope, as the years passed and he ran out of reasons to distrust his father, that one day I would be permitted to enter.

For much of this time, the Empire was at war. Shortly after being recalled from Italy, Belisarius was sent to fight the Sassanids. Under the leadership of their cruel and ambitious ruler, Nurshivan, the Sassanid armies had burst over our eastern frontiers like the pent-up waters of a great dam, flooding Roman territories and threatening to overrun the whole of Syria.

The Roman general entrusted with the defence of the region, Buzes, collected his forces at Hierapolis. After making a speech, exhorting the soldiers and citizens to fight to the last, he fled at night with a few attendants, leaving them to face the fury of the Sassanid host. Hierapolis fell, and the great city of Antioch, and many other Roman towns and cities.

Dire rumours reached Constantinople of the fate of our citizens in the East. Nurshivan was a merciless pagan savage, and committed terrible massacres, regardless of age or sex or degree. After the destruction of Antioch he stripped naked and bathed in the waters of the Orontes, as if to say this was his territory now, and he might do as he wished.

"Only one man can halt the progress of Nurshivan," said Procopius over dinner one evening, "Justinian knows that, and will pack Belisarius off to the East without delay. He is taking me with him, so we may not see other again for a while."

He was still a friend, and occasionally visited us when he could spare the time. Belisarius owned an estate at Rufinianae, barely a mile from my house. Procopius usually resided there, attending on his master and secretly working on his own history of our times.

This was a year after the end of the Italian war. I had not seen Procopius since leaving Italy, and a definite change had been wrought in him. He was always lean, and full of manic energy, but now there was something else: a kind of desperate, feverish intensity that seemed to be eating away at him from inside.

"You don't look well, my friend," I remarked, which was an understatement. He looked half-starved. The tendons on his scrawny neck stood out, and there was not an ounce of spare flesh on him. He picked restlessly at his food, speaking too quickly and eating too little.

"I am perfectly well," he snapped, "never better – never better! It is the Empire that sickens. Can you not see it, Coel? Can you not smell it? The stench of decay and corruption. It is all around us. It hangs in the air over this benighted city like a cloud, carrying plague and damnation and hellfire. Hellfire!"

His knife stabbed at a slice of chicken, missed, and almost overturned his bowl.

"You still can't wield a blade, then," I said drily, and was gratified to hear Arthur laugh. We were alone, just the three of us, seated on couches in the triclinium of my modest house.

Procopius sniffed, and crammed the morsel of chicken into his mouth. "You may jest," he grumbled, still chewing, "but it is the laughter of the damned. So might the Greeks have laughed while Athens burned, or the citizens of Carthage, even as Scipio's legions battered down their gates."

Arthur sat upright on his couch and peered out of the window, which commanded a good view of the Bosphorus. "I see no enemy fleets sailing up the Horn," he said lightly, "should we sound the alarm? Is the city threatened with imminent invasion?"

Procopius frowned horribly, stretching the too-tight yellow skin of his face. "Ignorant boy," he snarled, "have you read no history? Every great empire eventually destroys itself from within."

He leaned in closer, until I could smell the foul taint on his breath. "The Eastern Empire will go the same way as the West," he hissed, "unless God sees fit to strike down Justinian and his whore of a wife. They are an evil couple, sent by the Devil to destroy the last outposts of civilisation with their venality and blatant injustices. Theodora has turned the imperial court into a simmering nest of slaves and vipers and profiteers – a veritable Sodom, the canker in the bosom of the Roman Empire!"

I held up my hand. "Enough," I said patiently, "I won't have that sort of talk in my house. It is treason."

He sneered at my cowardice. "I seem to recall you were happy enough to commit treason in Italy."

"I made a mistake. Belisarius lied to me, and I was fool enough to believe him. Afterwards, I swore to never again put my faith in so-called great men, or dip my toe in politics. I'm sorry, Procopius. If you speak of such matters again, I will have you ejected from my house."

He growled and mumbled for a bit, but made no objection when I steered the conversation into calmer waters: the weather, my recent profits, the lamentable state of a recent shipload of mares from Hippo Regius.

Procopius' illness and foul temper stemmed from his disappointment in Belisarius. Like me, he had trusted the general, and hoped he would restore the former glory of the decaying Roman state. Belisarius' military victories had blinded us to the weaknesses of the man.

He continued to adore his wife, even though her affair with Theodosius had become the scandal of the age, and in doing so made himself ridiculous. The conqueror of North Africa and Italy, reduced to a hapless cuckold.

Fortune had deserted him. His reward for his loyalty in Italy was to be despatched to the East with a small and inadequate army. He had won great victories against the odds before, but Nurshivan was no fool, and refused to encounter the Romans in the field.

With half a mind on his wife's infidelity, Belisarius fought a desultory campaign. He eventually managed to push the Sassanids back into their own country, and bring Nurshivan to the negotiating table. A treaty was signed, whereby the Sassanid king promised not to attack Roman territory for five years.

The wax was hardly cooled before Belisarius hurried back to Constantinople, to finally confront his faithless wife. I had forbade Procopius from uttering treason in my house, but it was difficult not to be fascinated by the morsels of court gossip and scandal he fed us.

"Belisarius is a broken man," he confided to us during one of his infrequent visits, "would you believe, while in the East he tried to cultivate the friendship of Photius! He imagined Photius would help him bring about the downfall of Theodosius. Oh yes, our golden general finally accepts the truth of his wife's infidelity. How he wept over her! It was pathetic to witness. Shameful. A great man and a great soldier, reduced to slavery by a woman."

Photius was the son of Antonina, a deceptively godlike young man who had done his best to kill me, in the days when I mattered to the great ones of the Empire. I was astonished to hear Belisarius had forged an alliance with such a worthless character.

"So low had he fallen," Procopius continued, "and has fallen lower still. I overheard his confrontation with Antonina."

"Eavesdropping," remarked Arthur. Procopius glowered at him, but went on with his tale.

"He accused her of betraying him, and making him a laughing stock. She stood firm against the assault, and responded with a sally of her own, claiming that Belisarius owed her his life and career. Justinian, she said, was unimpressed with her husband's performance in the East, and had been on the verge of recalling him and accusing him of treason."

"Only Antonina's intervention – so she said, with that winning smile of hers – had persuaded the Emperor to relent, and saved Belisarius' head."

I could well imagine Antonina playing our endlessly suspicious little Emperor like a lyre, but thought Belisarius far too shrewd to be manipulated.

"Surely he did not believe it?" I exclaimed, "Justinian would not dare touch Belisarius. The general commands the loyalty of the army, and the love of the people."

Procopius bared his yellowing teeth. "I told you, he is a broken man. He not only believed it, but was beside himself with gratitude. He actually went down on his knees before Antonina and licked her feet! Imagine it, Coel, the man we followed through seven kinds of Hell in all those campaigns, abasing himself like a frightened slave before his own wife!"

I could scarcely credit any of it. Procopius was a bitter and disillusioned man, and probably guilty of exaggeration, but he told the truth in one respect. The star of Belisarius was gradually falling.

It disgusted me, to think of my old chief reduced to such a condition, but told myself it was none of my affair. He had made the great decision of his life at Ravenna, and was now suffering the consequences.

Years passed. The Emperor and his courtiers continued to plot and conspire against each other, and my business continued to prosper. Arthur married a sweet-faced young girl named Flavia, the daughter of a minor nobleman, and I looked forward to a gradual slide into peaceful old age.

In my heart, I knew I was allowing myself to be deceived. There would be no hearth and home for me in my old age, no laughter of grandchildren. Those who carry Arthur's blood are not suffered to rest.

I knew the end was coming when news reached Constantinople of a massive uprising in Italy. Roman rule was precarious, and the men Belisarius left behind to govern the country had failed to stamp out the stubborn embers of Gothic resistance.

By now Vitiges was dead, having expired in honourable captivity in Constantinople. Instead of submitting, the Goths had chosen a new leader. The Roman armies in Italy had already suffered defeats at his hands, and he was said to have raised enough men to threaten Florence.

His name passed through the streets of Constantinople like an evil rumour, or a portent of dread.

Totila.

21.

All manner of stories circulated about the new King of the Goths. Some said he was the product of a tryst between a German witch and the Devil, and carried the marks to prove it: a pair of horns, sharp fangs in place of teeth, nails like curving daggers, and other such nonsense. Others claimed he had unearthly powers, and was capable of raising dead warriors to life with a snap of his fingers.

In reality Italy was not being overrun by an army of the undead led by a witch-king, but a resurgent nation in arms led by a fierce and charismatic young nobleman. He was clever, too, and whipped up support by liberating slaves and distributing land to peasants.

His army, small at first, performed daring raids on Roman garrison troops, ambushing our patrols and plundering convoys before vanishing back into the hills and forests of northern Italy.

"The wretched man must be caught, and soon," said Procopius, "before these little victories start turning into major ones. Rome can ill-afford to fight another Spartacus."

"A few battered patrols and burned wagons don't amount to much," I said complacently, "Constantian and Alexander will bring this Totila and his little army of rebels to battle soon enough, and there will be an end of the matter."

Constantian and Alexander were the Roman generals Belisarius had left in charge of Italy. I didn't know much about Constantian, but Alexander was notorious. A former financial official turned soldier, who had distinguished himself by accusing the Roman army of defrauding the state. He tried to save money by slashing the wages of the soldiers in Italy, abolishing the free corn ration to the poor in Rome, and levying crushing taxes on towns and cities.

Unsurprisingly, Alexander was also hugely unpopular, and I confidently expected him to be murdered sooner rather than later. Not, however, before he and his colleague had dealt with the rebels.

Word of the fateful battle reached Constantinople on a suitably gloomy, overcast day, borne by an envoy in a single leaking galley crawling up the Bosphorus. The envoy had been wounded in the fighting, and gave a vivid account of it to the crowds gathered on the harbour.

"I escaped the slaughter with this," he cried, pointing dramatically at the bloodstained bandage wrapped round his head, "but thousands of our brave soldiers were not so fortunate. O Romans, was there ever such a defeat as this? Even Hannibal, whose name still carries a ring of terror down the centuries, never inflicted such shame on Roman arms."

"Get on with it," shouted Arthur, who had accompanied me to the harbour. Other impatient voices rose in agreement, and the pale-faced envoy hurried on with his narrative.

"As I say, twelve thousand of our finest soldiers marched from Ravenna to crush the ignoble Goths and their upstart princeling. They marched on Verona, but lately seized by the enemy, and retook the town by a clever stratagem at dead of night. One Artabazes, a Persian in our service, distinguished himself in this fight."

"Bugger Persians," someone yelled, "what about our lads? One of my sons is out there, serving in the army."

The envoy scowled. "Alas, our generals failed to press the advantage," he continued, "and Verona was lost again the very next day. Our army retreated to Faenza, to await the assault of the Goths."

The rest made for grim listening. Totila's army was roughly half the size of ours, but they fought like men inspired, led by their warlike chief on a massive white horse.

"He wore gold-plated armour, shining like the sun," the envoy claimed, "and wielded a lance with expert skill. Every time his lance struck, a Roman died."

It seemed our troops withstood the first wild charge of the Goths, but their morale was sapped by the mindless avarice of Alexander, who had seen fit to cut their pay again before the battle.

"When a band of three hundred Gothic cavalry suddenly appeared, charging into the rear of the Roman army, all discipline and valour was cast to the wind. Our men scattered and were mown by the pursuing Goths, who took the opportunity to exact bloody revenge for all their past defeats".

The envoy finished his account with a flourish. "The survivors fled to the nearest Roman outposts, where they holed up in terror of the enemy. Brave men, reduced to so many frightened mice by a single defeat!"

There were cries of anger and dismay among the crowd, and loud demands for something to be done – a familiar wail, one I had heard too many times to take much notice of. Those who uttered it were seldom the ones ordered to buckle on sword and shield and march away to salvage Rome's bruised national pride.

Arthur's reaction surprised me. His usual easy demeanour had vanished, and he was visibly upset, fists clenched, tears sparkling in his green eyes.

"Rome must hit back," he said through gritted teeth, "with everything we have.

Troops, ships, money. All our resources must be pooled towards smashing the Goths!"

"I didn't know you loved Rome so much," I replied, though it was a welcome glimpse into my son's state of mind.

Embarrassed, he hurriedly wiped away his tears and stalked away. I battled a rising tide of anxiety as I watched him go.

Arthur was the descendent of a long line of warriors, and now his hereditary instincts were coming to the fore. I had done my best to dissuade him from joining the army, but always suspected my efforts were in vain. The day would come when the call of the trumpets would prove too strong for him to ignore.

"Not yet," I muttered, hastening after him, "not yet."

It was selfish, but I was determined not to lose my only child. There had rarely been any harsh words between us, but that night we argued into the small hours. His heart was set on joining the cavalry, and I used every low stratagem I could think of to stop him.

"Think of your wife," I cried, pointing to the ceiling. Flavia, sensing the tension between her husband and father-in-law, had retired to bed early. "She is with child. For their sake, if not mine, you cannot leave now."

Flavia was indeed carrying my grandchild, though another eight months would elapse before the infant came into the world. Arthur seemed strangely indifferent to his wife's condition, and had greeted the news of her pregnancy with a rather forced display of joy.

"It will be difficult for Flavia, I accept," he replied sullenly, "but she will suffer no more than any other soldier's wife. How can I stay here, growing rich and fat, while thousands of my fellow countrymen are fighting and dying in Italy?"

I ventured to approach him and lay a fatherly hand on his shoulder. "Listen to me," I said earnestly, "you may think this hypocrisy, coming from me, but the Romans are not your fellow countrymen. We are imperial citizens, yes, and I served for a number of years in the Roman army. But we are British. The blood of Nennius and Coel Hen runs in our veins. You owe Rome taxes, but not your life."

Arthur frowned down at me from his great height. Constant exercise with horses and a good diet had filled out his spare frame, and he had grown into a big, powerful young man.

In short, he was my grandsire come again. In my mind's eye I could easily picture him on the ridge at Mount Badon, rallying the British troops for a final charge, the Pendragon banner rippling above his head.

I shook away the image. This Arthur would live out his days in peace and comfort, not end them on some stricken battlefield, betrayed by his own kin.

"I want to do my duty," he said, though some of the passion had gone out of his voice.

I patted his brawny shoulder. "So you shall. Your duty is here, with your family. Let Italy take care of itself. This Totila won't last long. Belisarius will crush him like the insect he is."

I expected the Emperor to react quickly to our defeat at Faenza, and sent his one brilliant general to Italy without delay. However, mean-minded and suspicious as ever, Justinian kept Belisarius in Constantinople, where he could be watched, and put his faith in the generals who had already failed him.

More distressing news flew across the Adriatic. Totila was conducting a brilliant campaign, gaining more battles and driving our forces out of Tuscany. He avoided our well-defended cities, especially ports, but instead concentrated on seizing control of the countryside. He moved fast, far too fast for our befuddled generals, always turning up where he was least expected, carrying out lethal raids and ambushes that sapped our strength and fed his legend.

I listened to the news of Totila's progress with mounting frustration. Though I had left the army behind, and Belisarius, it still filled me with anger to hear of how all our conquests were being thrown away, like good grain from a sack, by the fools and incompetents we had left to guard Italy.

"God and all the Saints," I shouted when I heard that virtually the whole of southern Italy had submitted to Totila, "what is happening out there? Where are our troops?"

"Running away, according to the latest reports," Arthur said gloomily, "or hiding behind strong walls. Totila avoids pitched battles, and our men are too frightened to make him fight one."

The news from Italy was dispiriting, but soon overwhelmed by private sorrows.

Flavia gave birth in late summer. The labour was harrowing, lasting almost twelve hours, during which time I sat downstairs with Arthur, drinking heavily and trying to block out the poor girl's shrieks.

"She was never strong," said Arthur, who also punished the wine, "I should have picked out some plump farmer's daughter from the hills. Wide hips and never a cross word."

The midwives did their best, but were unable to save the child. My granddaughter was stillborn. Her pitiful little body lies buried in the great cemetery on the Western side of the Bosphorus. The tiny grave is marked by a white marble cross, upon which is inscribed her name:

ELLIFER

My mother's name. Perhaps it was blasphemy to give a name to one who never drew the breath of life, but in my grief I cared nothing for the condemnation of the church.

Flavia barely survived the trauma of childbirth, and was broken in spirit by the loss of her child. I feared Arthur might not comfort her, but he was kind in his way, and stayed by his wife's bedside until her strength returned.

Our house was a sad, melancholy place, haunted by the ghost of the dead girl. In the midst of all this, when every day was a trial to be endured, a most unexpected visitor arrived at my door.

My old chief, Belisarius.

22.

He came alone, which was dangerous for a
man in his position, with so many enemies,
and dressed in a plain grey woollen tunic and
brown hooded mantle.

I had not seen the general, save from afar
during parades, for over four years. Our last
meeting had been in Ravenna, when he
apologised for his deceit and permitted me to
retire from the army.

My servant informed me there was a man at
the door who insisted on seeing the master of
the house. I was in my private study at the
time, next to my bedchamber, trying and
failing to work on a set of accounts for the
previous month. Thoughts of my dead
grandchild clawed at me, and the painful
memory of her funeral.

"Did he give a name?" I snapped.

"No, sir," the servant replied, "but he claims
to be an old soldier, who served with you in
Africa and Italy."

I rubbed my eyes, sore from hours of staring
at numbers. This wasn't the first time some
down-at-heel veteran had visited my house,
claiming to be a comrade of mine from the
wars. I found it difficult to turn them away,
these crippled old beggars, cast aside by the
state after their usefulness was expended. My
clerk disapproved, but more often than not I

ended up giving them a purse of money and a few kind words.

"Ah, show him in," I said, pushing away the rolls of parchment on my desk, "and fetch a jug of wine and two cups. The cheap stuff, mind."

Moments later, an imposing figure stood framed in the doorway. I had expected the usual skulking, whining beggar, probably missing some body part or other, but this man had a presence about him.

His face was yet hidden under the hood. "Well, Coel," said a strangely familiar voice.

My servant had already brought the wine. I smiled up at the figure in the doorway, and poured two generous measures.

There was a sheathed dagger in the left-hand drawer of my desk. "Come in, come in," I said jovially, inching my left hand closer to the drawer, "I see you know my name. Might I ask yours?"

"Flavius Belisarius," said the other man, pushing back his hood.

I froze. The man standing before me was recognisably Belisarius, though his face had aged considerably since I last saw it at close quarters. His thinning black hair was rubbed away completely from the top of his scalp, and his close-shaved beard was now almost entirely grey.

Belisarius was always an aesthetic-looking man, more priest than soldier by appearance.

The deep lines at the corners of his mouth and eyes had proliferated, and the weathered skin was stretched too tight over his long, narrow skull. He looked like a man who knew too much, worked too hard for little reward, and scarcely enjoyed a moment's comfort or peace of mind.

"General," I said, resisting the urge to stand up and salute, "you…you look well."

He smiled bleakly at the lie. "I am what God has made me. And the Emperor."

Feeling foolish, I gestured at a spare seat. "Please, sit down. Share a cup of wine with me."

"No, no," he said, waving away the courtesy, "I will not presume on your hospitality any longer than necessary. I feared you might turn me away."

I groped for words. "The world moves on," I said weakly, "and we must move with it. I should feel grateful for what passed in Ravenna."

"You have certainly prospered since," he replied, "and breed the finest horses in the city, so they say. I have considered purchasing some of your stock. At a discount, I hope."

"General," I said, rubbing my head, which was beginning to pound, "am I to understand you have come here to discuss business?"

"Of a sort."

He clasped his hands together and stood quiet for a few seconds, gazing at the floor.

"Caesar is sending me back to Italy, at last," he said, "the situation there is intolerable. I daresay you know something about it."

I nodded. "Totila has captured Beneventum, and now threatens Naples. He has to be stopped."

"Just so. I am gathering all my veterans about me before sailing. Every man will be needed. Coel, will you take up your grandsire's sword again?"

It was rank discourtesy to drink when a guest went dry, but I had a sudden thirst. Half a cupful of rough red wine vanished down my throat before I gave him an answer.

"Caledfwlch has hung over my fireplace for four years," I said, wiping my mouth, "and is destined to stay there. I bear you no ill-will, general, but meant what I said at Ravenna. I am retired."

I gave silent thanks that Arthur was not present, but down on the harbour, overseeing the unloading of a consignment of foals from Carthage. He would have leaped at the chance to escape my house, and all the gloom and misery that had descended on it.

"You don't need an old man like me," I continued, "God's bones, I am almost fifty! What use would I be, save to look after remounts?"

Belisarius was four or five years my junior, though he looked at least a decade older. "The best soldiers mature with age," he said, "like a fine wine."

He glanced meaningfully at the rotgut I was drinking. I could not help but laugh.

"It's no good, sir," I said, "you can't get round me. I pray you win a crushing victory in Italy, and bring Totila back in chains. Better yet, leave his body in Italy and present his head in a casket to the Emperor. But the army will have to cope without my presence."

"Or my son's," I added before he could speak again, "I stay in Constantinople, and Arthur stays with me."

A note of desperation entered his voice. "Coel, I will have great need of loyal officers about me in Italy."

"I'm sure you can find some," I replied carelessly, "how many men is the Emperor giving you?"

He took a deep breath. "None."

"What?"

"After our recent defeats, Caesar claims he has no troops to spare. I am to sail to Italy with as many of veterans as I can collect, and there try to raise an army from native volunteers."

It was monstrous. Of all Justinian's petty acts of treachery towards Belisarius, this was the worst. It was true Rome had suffered severe losses, including the destruction of a fleet carrying reinforcements off the Bay of

Naples, but fresh troops could always be raised or hired.

The sickening truth hit me like a blow. Justinian was deliberately sending his greatest general to die. An honourable death in battle against overwhelming numbers of barbarians. He wanted him out of the way, without risking the scandal of a trial and public execution. Belisarius was still far too popular for that.

This, mark you, was the man whom Belisarius had refused to betray! Justinian's ignoble fear and envy of the general was only fuelled by the knowledge Belisarius had been in a position to destroy him. Hence he schemed and pondered on ways of bringing down the one loyal servant he should have esteemed above all others.

For a brief moment I was tempted to accept the general's invitation. If he had offered to lead a rebellion against the Emperor, and storm the Great Palace at the head of his Veterans, I might well have done so.

I pushed aside temptation. It was too late. Far too late.

"I'm sorry, sir," I said without meeting his eye, "my prayers shall go with you, but that is all."

23.

Knowing it would inflame his martial instincts, I kept the visit of Belisarius a secret from my son. Arthur's duty, as I saw it, was to stay in Constantinople and tend to his wife. She, poor, broken-hearted creature, was much affected by the loss of their child, and I despaired of her recovery.

My cause was not helped by the constant flow of desperate news from Italy. Belisarius sailed to Ravenna with the tiny handful of soldiers allowed him, and set about raising an army of four thousand volunteers from the natives. With this enthusiastic rabble at his back, he advanced boldly to meet the resurgent Goths.

The ensuing campaign was a confused series of disasters and victories. Hopelessly outnumbered, betrayed and let down time and again by his generals, Belisarius somehow managed to relieve some beleaguered Roman towns and fortresses, and worst the Goths in a few minor skirmishes.

For all that, his efforts to scrape together a proper army came to nothing. Dismayed by the endless run of defeats, and enraged by the constant slashing of their wages, a good portion of the imperial troops in Italy deserted the eagle and offered their swords to Totila. Unable to meet the Goths in battle, Belisarius sent a desperate message to the Emperor, pleading for aid:

"Great prince, I am arrived in Italy, unprovided with men or money, with horses or with arms, nor can any spirit bear up against such disadvantages as these….were it sufficient for success that Belisarius should appear in Italy, your aim would be accomplished. I am now in Italy. But if you desire to conquer; far greater preparations must be made; and the title of general dwindles to a shadow, where there is no army to uphold it…"

True to his nature and inclination, Justinian ignored the plea, and sent no aid. The fortunes of Totila continued to wax, as did the numbers of his army, and city after city fell to him.

At last, thanks to the treachery of the garrison, he seized Rome, and the Eternal City was once again in the hands of barbarians. Belisarius arrived too late with his fleet to save the city, and was forced to withdraw with the mocking laughter of Gothic warriors ringing in his ears.

I retired to my study when I heard the news, and wept tears of futile rage. The grotesque shades of all my dead comrades, who had fought alongside me on the walls of Rome and given their lives to defend the city, haunted my dreams: cursing me for a coward and a traitor, who had failed to answer the call to arms when it came.

If I had one consolation in this grim time, it was the knowledge that the Empress was dying. The details from the palace were unclear, but it seemed Theodora had contracted some kind of suppurating ulcer or tumour, which her physicians were powerless to remedy.

I was told she died slowly, and in the most exquisite pain. When she finally gave up the ghost, and the doleful lamentation of her priests echoed through the streets, I drank a quiet toast to my childhood friend Felix, whom Theodora had murdered for no other reason than to spite me.

Justinian was said to be prostrate with grief, and I earnestly hoped he would soon follow his evil consort to the grave.

"Let him die, lord," I prayed in the lonely silence of my bedchamber, "and keep Theodora company in the deepest furnace of Hell."

Frustratingly, the Emperor did not die, but limped on, an increasingly forlorn and despised figure. Deaf to the frantic entreaties of Belisarius, he allowed himself to become embroiled in arguments with churchmen and theologians, and treated the war in Italy as an irritating distraction.

The sorry campaign drew to a miserable and shameful end for Rome. Belisarius was recalled, again on the pretext of being needed in the East, and after his departure the whole of Italy was lost to Totila. Most of our remaining garrisons were exterminated, and the native Italians – the same people had cheered the arrival of our fleet from Sicily, just a few years previously – hailed the all-conquering Gothic king as their new sovereign.

I might have ended my days in Constantinople, grumbling, as old soldiers do, over the follies of their superiors, but largely content. I was not short of worldly wealth, and I still had my son.

I was deceived. God, as I have said, allows the blood of Arthur no rest.

In the deep winter of the year five hundred and fifty, in the twenty-third year of Justinian's reign, Flavia was brought to bed of another child.

I had advised them not to try again. Flavia was weakened by the previous tragedy, and I feared her insides were damaged.

Arthur would not listen to me, and Flavia meekly obeyed her husband's wishes. He was determined to have a son, to carry on the unbroken blood-line of British princes.

"Before God, I regret I ever told you of your ancestry," I said bitterly, "I would rather see your wife alive, and happy, than risk her for the sake of our family. The line of kings was broken long ago, Arthur. Even your great-grandsire never laid claim to a crown."

He proved stubborn, and I wondered if Elene's shade was working through him, exacting her long-delayed vengeance on me.

If so, she got her wish. Flavia endured another excruciating labour, and produced another stillborn child. To twist the knife in Arthur's wound, the child was another daughter.

This time, there was nothing the Greek physician and midwives we had hired could do to save Flavia. She would not stop bleeding, and died in the small hours of the morning, without seeing the pathetic fragment of dead flesh she had brought into the world.

24.

My son was a changed man after the death of his wife. For three days and nights after the funeral he kept to his room, refusing to eat or drink or speak to anyone. When he emerged, drawn and haggard and with a world of pain in his eyes, the bright youth I had known was quite gone.

I was surprised by the depth of his grief, since he never seemed to care overmuch for Flavia in life. Like his mother, Arthur possessed depths and twists to his character I was incapable of divining.

With nothing left to keep him in Constantinople, he revived his ambition to join the army. "You cannot persuade me otherwise this time," he said as he broke his three-day fast, "I need to get away from this city and all its ghosts."

There was iron resolution in his voice, and I lacked the will to fight him. Flavia's death, and the loss of my second grandchild, had opened fresh wounds in my battered soul.

"You must do whatever you think is right," I replied, "whatever your decision, you have my blessing."

After he had forced down a morsel of bread, he went to the fireplace and took down Caledfwlch. The sword had hung there for many years. I had not touched it since. Nor had anyone save the servant tasked with polishing the blade and keeping it sharp.

"It has a weight to it," he said, running his hand gently along the blade.

"The weight of souls," I replied, "of blood and death. Caledfwlch has ushered hundreds of men into the next world."

I looked at the thing with distaste, and a twinge of fear. Once precious to me, my grandsire's sword was now a reminder of past terrors and disappointments. I was still plagued with dreams of slaughter, half-buried memories of the battles I had witnessed in Africa and Italy.

"All those dead men," I said, "and for what? Belisarius may as well have stayed at home and grown cabbages. All his victories and conquests have crumbled away like a hollow pile of sand."

"That is the truth of war, my son. Men march away, and not all of them come back. They leave nothing but shallow graves, mourning widows and fatherless children."

Arthur held Caledfwlch up to the light streaming in through a latticed window. "A grave for Constantine," he said, "a grave for Aurelius; a grave for Uther. All the world's wonder, no grave for Arthur!"

He was reciting a snatch of verse I had taught him, long ago. I got it from some of the Germanic mercenaries in the Roman army, who in turn heard it from their kin in Britain.

Arthur, the enemy of their race, who had piled up heaps of their slain at Mount Badon, was now one of their heroes. All the world, it seemed, was embracing the tales of my famous ancestor.

"I care not where they bury me," my son said, with more than a trace of bitterness, "let me rot on some distant battlefield. The ravens can pick at my bones. As for my wife and children, they have gone before."

"But I have not," I said quietly.

For the first and perhaps only time, I managed to inspire a little pity in him. He returned Caledfwlch to its hook and caught me in a fierce embrace.

"I will make you proud, father," he whispered. I wanted to reply that he already had, but the breath was crushed from my lungs.

Arthur took to training with the citizen levies, who drilled regularly on the plains outside the city walls. I was unsurprised to hear he excelled at every form of weapons exercise, as well as horsemanship, and drew praise from the tough veterans who oversaw the drill.

Meanwhile the Emperor was seized by a rare burst of energy and competence. He shook off his mourning for Theodora, put aside his wrangling theologians, and took measures to reverse the catastrophe in Italy.

Still, nothing on earth could persuade him to restore Belisarius to rank and favour. The general was detained in Constantinople, a free man but constantly under the shadow of imperial displeasure, spared from destruction only thanks to his wife, who exerted a strange influence over Justinian.

Having put aside his only great general, Justinian cast about for someone to replace him. First he chose his nephew Germanus, then changed his mind in favour of Liberius, a decrepit civilian with no military experience, then to an Armenian named Artaban, then back to Germanus.

"Vacillating ninny," sneered Procopius, who had returned to Constantinople with his master, "he will end up appointing his horse as commander-in-chief. A dumb beast can scarce be a worse choice than Liberius."

Eventually Justinian settled on his nephew, and sent him to Sicily with a fleet. Germanus had a mixed reputation, having fought well against the rebels in North Africa, but fled before the fury of the Sassanids when they descended on Antioch. Justinian had succeeded in marrying him off to Matasontha, the ex-Queen of the Goths, so he also enjoyed some popularity among her people.

"Germanus will fail," Procopius said confidently, "Totila will give him a good thrashing, and he will run back to uncle with his tail between his legs."

"I want to join the army bound for Sicily," Arthur announced. Procopius, who was fond of my son, stared at him in horror.

"Don't be so damned stupid," he rasped, "you may as well fall on that old sword now and save yourself the trouble. Germanus won't achieve a thing."

In the event, Germanus died, of a fever he picked up in Sicily. Plunged back into the depths of grief by this unexpected loss, Justinian was driven to extremity, and chose for his general an ageing, deceitful, twisted little half-man.

"Narses!" Procopius informed us, almost choking on his mirth, "he is going to send Narses to rescue Italy! Now may God help Rome, for the Emperor has failed her."

25.

I was appalled by the Emperor's decision, and tried to forbid Arthur from joining the army. Any campaign led by Narses, I argued, could only end in total disaster.

"He is a crippled eunuch, a greasy, shamelessly corrupt courtier, a master of wiles and treachery and every foul trick," I said forcefully, "the little bastard can't even ride, with his twisted legs, but has to be carried everywhere in a litter! A fine leader, to take a Roman army into the field! Are we to rely on the Goths laughing themselves to death when they set eyes on him?"

Arthur was unmoved. He was twenty-six years old now, in the prime of youth and manhood, and this was his time.

"You can forbid me nothing, father," he said calmly, "though I honour you for your love and concern. I will go to Italy, with or without your blessing or permission."

I am not a demonstrative man, but his icy stubbornness drove me into a rage. I raged and cursed, and broke furniture, and threatened to have him clapped in irons if he refused to listen to reason.

Arthur waited patiently for the storm to blow itself out. I may as well have expended my wrath on a statue, for all the effect I had on him.

For a moment I despaired, but then an idea struck me. "Very well," I said, when I had control of myself again, "if you go, I go."

Arthur was rarely taken aback, but I was gratified to see him blink. "What? You mean to join the army again? Father, you are too old."

"And," he added, poking me in the belly, "too fat. Fine living has been the ruin of you."

Insolent whelp. If he wasn't quite so big, I would have taken my belt to him.

"I would never re-enlist," I said, thinking myself very cunning, "but the army will need horses. Lots of horses. No doubt a good part of our stock will be requisitioned. I mean to take them myself, and see the poor beasts are not ill-used. We paid good money for them, after all."

He looked at me incredulously. "You, who once commanded Roman troops in the field, mean to follow the army as a horse-trader?"

"Why not?" I shrugged, "or a quartermaster, maybe. Even a cook. An army marches on its stomach."

"Not for long, if exposed to your culinary skills," he retorted, but there was nothing he could say or do to stop me. We had reached an impasse, and had to make the best of it.

Since Arthur was set on joining the army, I tried to secure a good berth for him. I still had some influence with certain high-ranking officers, old comrades from the wars, and exerted it to get him into the cavalry.

This presented little difficulty. Arthur was the very image of a promising young officer, and rode as well as anyone. He was appointed a centenar, in command of a hundred Herulian horsemen. This was my choice. I knew the Heruls well, their customs and fighting style, from my time in their camp.

"They are a rough lot, with some strange beliefs you must never try to change or interfere with," I advised my son, "above all, they respect courage and horsemanship. Lead from the front, try not to fall off your horse, and you should deal very well with them."

The preparations for the campaign were encouraging, and revealed the extent of Justinian's perfidy towards Belisarius. Narses, having witnessed the general's fate in Italy, refused to accept the command unless given adequate supplies of men and money.

Justinian refused his favourite nothing. He emptied the imperial coffers to please him, raising levies from Thrace and Illyria, six thousand Lombard mercenaries hired from their King, Alboin, and three thousand Herulian cavalry. To these were added further auxiliaries, hired at Narses' personal expense, and even a detachment of Sassanids, refugees who had deserted Nurshivan and fled into imperial territory to escape his wrath.

In all, the army amounted to no less than thirty thousand men, twice the size of anything Belisarius was ever entrusted with. With such a host at his command, he might have achieved his dream of re-conquering the entire Western Empire, and raised the name of his Emperor to deathless heights of glory. But Justinian was not the man to realise such ambitions. The brief moment passed, and I believe the empire will never recover its old power and prestige.

Narses surprised me. Twelve years had passed since he briefly led a small Roman army in Italy. Since then he had done no soldiering (unless playing chess counts) and showed no obvious interest in reviving his military career.

Now, handed a fresh opportunity by Justinian, he threw himself into the task with a skill and energy I would have thought beyond him. Perhaps he had spent his time devouring the histories of old wars, but his conduct of the early stages of the campaign could not be faulted.

The Goths controlled the seas off the east coast of Italy, so there was no chance of launching another seaborne invasion. Instead Narses ordered the army to march to Salona, an ancient city on the Dalmatian coast, and from there to the head of the Adriatic Gulf. It was a long march, but meant the army could invade Gothic territory from the north, avoiding their fleet.

During all the bustle and preparations for war, Narses found time to send me a brief note. It arrived at my house, carried by an insouciant Egyptian slave, as I was making my final arrangements for departure:

I knew you would serve me at the last. Congratulations on the appointment of your son. I will observe his progress with great interest.
- Narses.

I scrunched the parchment into a ball, dropped it on the ground and crushed it underfoot.

"There is my reply," I said, grinning up at the Egyptian. He returned the grin with interest.

"My master warned me you might not be polite," he said, "especially when I repeat the verbal part of my message. When we reach Salona, you and your son are to join our fleet stationed there."

"What fleet?" I demanded, "my understanding was that the army would march north and invade Italy by land."

"And so it shall. But it will take many months to reach the Gulf, and the Goths are already blockading our last ports on the Italian mainland. They must not be allowed to fall."

"Croton and Ancona," I said. He gracefully nodded his sleek, perfumed head before continuing.

"Just so. Totila is most impertinent. Even now, fifty of his warships blockade Ancona, while some three hundred other vessels are raiding the coast of Epirus and the Ionian Islands."

"And I'm supposed to stop him, am I?"

The envoy gave a mannered little chuckle. "No, no, though your contribution is appreciated. My master has ordered forty Roman ships to muster at Salona. They will sail to engage the Gothic fleet at Ancona, and on the way be reinforced by ships from Ravenna."

In spite of all our losses in Italy, we had at least managed to hold onto Ravenna, the capital.

"I still fail to see why my presence is required," I said, "or my son's. He is a captain of horse, and we are both quite useless at sea. Who commands the fleet from Ravenna?"

"Valerian."

I vaguely knew of him, a tough and capable veteran, and one of the few to serve Belisarius faithfully in Italy.

"And at Salona?"

The envoy's smoothly handsome face split into an infuriating smirk.

"John the Sanguinary."

26.

I tried to comfort myself. After ten years it seemed unlikely that John still held a grudge against me, especially since he had risen high in the Emperor's favour, whereas I had sank into obscurity.

Besides, Arthur was right. I was fat, and fifty, and badly out of condition from my shameful habit of gorging at table. The long, weary march from Salona to the Gulf, through the disease-ridden Dalmatian marshes, was not a happy prospect.

Nor could I disobey orders. If not a soldier, I was still in the service of Rome, and Narses was the commander-in-chief. He might have had me killed at any time, if he so wished, but instead preferred to torment me from afar. Such was the price I paid for refusing to desert Belisarius for his service, all those years ago.

"I am in for a sea-voyage," I informed Arthur, "with a battle at the end of it."

He paled. Like me, he loathed and dreaded the sea. "To what end?" he demanded, "my Heruls are no use at sea. They will be needed to fight the Goths in Perugia."

I smiled bleakly. Narses had thought of everything, and his slave had furnished me with all the details before leaving my house.

"You are to stay with the army," I explained, "but I am needed to help relieve Ancona. The garrison has been under siege for months. They are running low on food, and taken to eating their horses. I am to sail with the fleet with my stock, to replace the animals lost to famine."

Arthur seemed lost. We had barely spent a day apart for over ten years, ever since I brought him to Constantinople. All that time I struggled to understand him, and we never grew as close as I would have liked, but he had come to rely on me.

"You wanted to go," I said, clasping his hand, "to prove yourself. Now is your opportunity. We shall meet again, when the army reaches Ravenna."

I tried to sound optimistic, but the chances of us meeting again were slender. The march from Salona, all the way around the Adriatic coast, would take many months, while our army would have to fight its way through hordes of Goths.

In addition, there was no guarantee our fleet would defeat Totila's. Both sides had an equal number of ships, and the Gothic admirals were said to be able men.

Our army marched from Constantinople, the first landward departure from the city I had experienced. The people gathered to cheer as our troops marched down the Mese with all the grand panoply of war, trumpets playing, cymbals clashing and banners waving.

My son took his place among the mounted Herulians in the vanguard, while I stayed far to the rear, riding in the back of a baggage wagon. From there I could keep a careful eye on my horses, over forty pureblood young stallions from Hispania, just recently broken.

The eyes of the people lining the streets were all for our soldiers. None paid any heed to me, the fat greybeard taking his ease on a straw bale in the back of a cart, but I carefully scanned the sea of faces. I was looking for Belisarius, wondering if he had ventured from his house in disguise, and come to watch the army march away.

"The army he should be leading," I muttered. There was no sign of his lean, bearded face among the crowds. Eventually I gave up and settled back to contemplate the heavens.

The army passed through the city's elaborate western defences, the old Constantinian Wall and then the double line of walls built by the Emperor Theodosius, and emerged from the Golden Gate. This was the main ceremonial entrance to the city, made from blocks of sparkling white marble in the form of a triumphal arch.

It was also the gate via which I had first entered Constantinople with my mother, almost forty-five years gone. As always, the thought of her filled me with sorrow. I closed my eyes until the wagon had rumbled well past the gate.

I would never see it, or the city, again.

The army marched on to Salona, through the bleak plains of Thrace, baked dry and hard by the summer sun. I was reminded me of the wastelands of Perugia, strangled by the heat while its people died of thirst and starvation. Fortunately our troops were well-supplied, and suffered none of the privations of previous campaigns.

After a two-week march, our army crossed into Dalmatia at a leisurely pace and reached Salona unscathed, without glimpsing any sign of the enemy. Dalmatia was once occupied by the Goths, but had abandoned much of the country and their troops to Italy, leaving just a few scattered garrisons. Occasionally we marched past one of their outposts, but the men inside wisely stayed behind their high walls and strong gates.

"Two hundred miles from Constantinople," grumbled Arthur after the army pitched camp a day's march from the coast, "and all I have to show for it is saddle sores. Caledfwlch is quiet in her scabbard."

"And will remain so for a while yet," I said cheerfully, "it is a long way to Italy. A very long way. At the speed Narses likes to march, the Goths may have died of old age before you reach Ravenna."

Steel hissed on oiled leather as Arthur slowly drew Caledfwlch. "You will see action before me," he said, offering me the sword, hilt-first, "perhaps you should take her back. She has never failed you in battle."

The blade of Caesar's sword gleamed in the half-darkness of early evening. For a second or two I was tempted. It would have been good to feel the worn ivory grip in my hand again, and the familiar weight and balance of the ancient gladius.

"No," I said, with a great effort of will, "I gave Caledfwlch away, and no longer have any right to it. A plain sword will serve me well enough. Assuming I can find the strength to fight, with a deck heaving under my feet."

The mere thought of fighting aboard ship was enough to make my stomach clench. I suspected Narses was aware of my sea-sickness, and wanted me to suffer vomiting and loose bowels while the battle raged around me.

Salona was a rich port, the capital of Dalmatia, and had remained loyal to Rome when the Goths overran the rest of the province. The landward gates stood open to welcome our troops, and imperial banners flew from the walls.

My guts gave a twinge when I spotted the masts of our ships clustered in the harbour. I counted thirty-six vessels in all, mostly war galleys, with a few smaller dromons and four fat-bottomed transport ships.

I made my way to the harbour, ignoring the puzzled and occasionally amused looks the citizens gave me. As old soldiers went, I was a fairly unimpressive specimen, puffing and sweating as I fought my way through the busy streets. I had struggled into my old armour – not the fine gear Belisarius gave me, which I had sold off, but a plain knee-length mail coat and a cavalry helmet with dangling cheek-pieces – and was feeling the strain of it, especially around the waist.

John the Sanguinary's flagship was docked nearest to the harbour, and the largest vessel in the fleet, a sleek war galley gleaming with fresh black and gold paint.

I smelled John before I saw him. He still doused himself in perfume, like a cheap dockside whore, and was standing among a little group of his cronies. Like their chief, all were resplendent in finely-wrought armour and costly silks, and carried expensive swords with gold hilts.

They were also notably young and tall and comely, as though chosen for their physical grace and ability to look grand in military uniform. Next to this pack of brightly coloured starlings, I was an old crow, drab and unsightly.

"Good to see you again, sir," I said in a loud voice, interrupting their banal chatter. John swung around, a look of annoyance on his darkly handsome features. He hadn't aged a day since I last met him, outside the gates of Rimini.

"Ah, the tame Briton," he said in that cold, sneering tone I remembered so well, "Narses told me to expect you. You have a few more grey hairs since we last met, and a bit of extra padding around the middle. Are you pregnant, man, or have you stuffed a cushion down there?"

His cronies laughed at the feeble jest and gave each other knowing looks. Their high-pitched braying grated on my nerves, but I did my best to ignore it.

"My horses are stationed outside the city, sir," I said patiently, "and are ready to embark whenever you choose."

"And? What is that to me? I am the admiral of the fleet, not a God-cursed beastmaster, and cannot attend to every minor detail. Have the animals loaded aboard the transports without delay."

I saluted and wandered away, feeling the heat of his gaze on my back. If he wanted to plunge a dagger into it, here was his opportunity.

As ever, I overrated my importance. John the Sanguinary cared little whether I lived or died, and the faint animosity between us was long-buried in the past. He was an anxious man, entrusted by Narses with the task of relieving the last two major Roman ports in Italy and destroying the Gothic fleet.

Narses' judgment could not usually be faulted, but I thought he had blundered in choosing John for his admiral, allowing friendship to blind him to the man's limitations. John was a cavalry officer, and a good one, but had no experience of naval warfare.

That evening I had the Devil's own job loading my horses aboard the transports, or rather my handlers did. I confined myself to standing on the jetty and cursing their incompetence while they laboured to get the terrified beasts into the barges.

Horses loathe the sea, almost as much as I do, and they had to be lifted aboard with a crane. Frantic with rage and terror, they kicked and bit and lashed out at the handlers, breaking one man's arm and shattering another's ribcage. Darkness had fallen before the thing was done, and I was obliged to pay for the injured men to be taken to a sanatorium.

Weary and footsore, I went in search of Arthur and found him eating supper with his men, on the outskirts of the city of white tents that had sprung up outside Salona.

I shared a cup of wine with him, complimented the good discipline and order of his men, and tried to put off the inevitable farewell.

Arthur did it for me. "Until Ravenna, then," he said suddenly, offering his hand.

I clasped it. "Until Ravenna," I replied, silently cursing the catch in my voice.

The rest of my night was spent in virtually sleepless dread, haunted by images of burning ships and myself drowning, clawing helplessly at the black waters as they closed over my head; or else visions of Arthur, lost on some misted battlefield, calling feebly for his parents even as his life-blood spilled from a mortal wound.

These merry thoughts occupied me until morning, when the brazen call of trumpets announced the imminent departure of the fleet. Valerian had arrived from Ravenna with his twelve ships, and we were now ready to sail.

"Glory and death," I muttered as I made my reluctant way down to the harbour, "God spare me from either."

27.

The familiar twinges of sickness descended on me before my transport had even crawled out of the harbour. She was an ugly, slow-moving vessel, and wallowed low in the water, thanks to the weight of supplies and animals packed into her hull. The terrified shrieking of my horses, cooped up in tiny pens below deck, did nothing to improve my condition.

"This ship is too full," I complained to the captain, a hard-faced Greek with a jagged scar where his nose used to be, "look how low she rides in the water. She may sink of her own accord without any aid from the Goths."

"Do your bit to lighten the load, then, you old bugger," he snarled, "and go and puke over the side. You look green enough. But you won't do it on my quarterdeck, you hear? Not if you want to keep the skin on your back."

I struggled down the ladder onto the maindeck and heaved my breakfast over the rail. A group of Cilician sailors stampeded past me, trailing onto the end of a rope and yelling at me to stand aside. I crouched against the side, hand clapped over my mouth, and waited for the boiling chaos in my guts to subside a little.

When I had recovered sufficiently, I stood on shaking legs and looked out to sea. The other transports were keeping pace with us, strung out in a line from north to south. They were also over-full, and laboured through the water with all the grace and speed of a pack of dying turtles.

The rest of the fleet were spread out to the north-west, and divided into squadrons, with the smaller dromons acting as escorts to the galleys. John's flagship was just visible, a lean black shape knifing easily through the sea at the head of the first squadron.

By my reckoning, Ancona lay more or less directly to the west. We were heading north-west, towards the region of Sena Gallica, a small port town on the Adriatic coast. Unsurprisingly, John the Sanguinary had not confided his battle-plan to me, but I guessed the Gothic fleet had been sighted there.

I remained at my post, rubbing my aching belly and silently begging God to restore my strength: enough, at least, to give a reasonable account of myself in the fight. Terrified of being dragged under if I fell into the sea, I had discarded my mail shirt, and for protection wore only my old cavalry helmet and an iron-rimmed buckler strapped to my left arm.

The Greek captain appeared at my side. "Recovered?" he asked.

"Not really," I replied with a grimace, "the sea has always been my bane. Poseidon must have a grudge against me."

He gave a mirthless little chuckle. "Got any more questions for me? I noticed you staring at the fleet."

I looked at him warily, but he seemed friendly enough, and not about to have the skin flayed from my back.

"Well," I said, pointing to the north, "shouldn't our galleys be reducing sail? At this rate we're going to be left behind."

The bulk of our fleet was indeed speeding away, towards the barely visible line of the Italian coast. It was a bright, blustery Autumn day, and the wind was in their favour.

"Yes," replied the captain, "won't we just?"

The hairs bristled on the back of my neck as the import of his words sank in. My reply was cut off as the damned ship gave a sudden lurch, almost bowling me off my feet.

His brawny arm shot out to seize my arm. "Steady," he said, "can't have you falling overboard. We'll have need of every man soon enough, even a sickly land-crawler like you."

"Bait," he added before I could ask the obvious question, "our admiral is dangling us before the Goths like a prime bit of meat, in the hope they snap us up."

I gaped at him, and at the distant blood-red sail of John's flagship.

"Bastard," I spat. He was deliberately sacrificing the transports, and me into the bargain.

In hindsight, his strategy was sound. John was directing the fleet according to his soldier's instincts, deliberately exposing his flank to lure the enemy into a fatal charge.

At the time, with my stomach churning and my blood boiling, I was in no mood to appreciate his clever tactics. The captain, on the other hand, appeared strangely indifferent.

"It was this, or hang," he said with a crooked grin, "me and my crew are all pirates, and should have gone to the gallows last week. John spared our lives on condition we took service aboard his death-ships."

"The other transports are the same," he added, "all crewed by the scum of the sea."

"If the Goths descend on us, we will all die," I said.

"Maybe. They might take us prisoner, or we can try and swim for it. We have a small chance. A better chance, at least, than the gallows offers."

I could do nothing but wait, stranded aboard the lumbering transport with its crew of condemned sea-rats. The remainder of our fleet was almost invisible now, a row of tiny sails bobbing on the far horizon to the north-west.

My hope was that the Goths would refuse John's bait. Another hour or so passed. I spent the time offering up multitudes of silent prayers, but God is endlessly fickle, and chose to ignore me.

"Enemy sighted!" bawled the look-out from his vantage point at the top of the mainmast, "off the port bow, there!"

I lurched across to the port side of the maindeck, and joined the crewmen staring out to sea, towards the west.

"Look there," growled a villainous-looking Cilician, all scars and stubble and barely suppressed aggression, "seven orange sails. Galleys, curse them, with a double bank of oars apiece."

I looked where he pointed, and saw them clear enough. Seven Gothic warships bearing down on us from the west. The wind was against them, but thanks to their oars they were still ploughing through the water at a fair speed.

I made some swift calculations. The enemy ships were of a roughly equal size to our galleys, and probably carried some two score fighting men apiece, besides the crew and oarsmen.

Our transports carried no more than twenty crewmen each. They were a tough-looking set, as pirates tend to be, but hopelessly outnumbered. We couldn't hope to make much of a fight of it.

The captain had no thoughts of surrender. "Don't just stand there gawping!" he bawled, "fetch your weapons, you misbegotten sons of pigs, and prepare to repel boarders!"

My heart sank as I watched his men scramble to arm. John hadn't supplied them with much – why bother wasting decent gear on the condemned? – and most could lay their hands on nothing better than a dagger and light throwing javelin. Five had bows and a sheaf of arrows apiece. There was no armour aboard, and only the captain and his first mate were fortunate enough to have helmets and shields.

I saw frantic activity aboard our fellow transports as the men aboard them prepared to die. The dry heaving in my guts was replaced by the familiar swelling of fear, and I badly needed to void my bladder.

Fear and a desire to piss were preferable to all-consuming sickness, and I felt some of my strength return. Not much, but enough to strike a blow or two before the end.

The steady thump-thump-thump of drums sounded across the water, pounding out the rhythm for the oarsmen aboard the Gothic ships. They were slaves, many of them Roman soldiers taken prisoner during the recent wars. Now they were forced to bring about the doom of their countrymen.

My heart thumped in time with the drums. I could seldom recall feeling so nervous before a fight, but I was ill, and old, and had not seen action for over ten years. Nor had I ever fought at sea, trying to keep my footing on the heaving deck of a ship.

"Javelin-men on the port side," the captain's harsh voice barked from above, "archers with me on the foredeck. Move, you steaming piles of dung."

Bare feet drummed across the planking of the deck as his crew rushed to obey. None seemed to care what I did, so I retreated to the mainmast and rested my back against the wood, hoping it would aid my balance.

Guttural yells and insults drifted across the water. The galleys were closing in, so near I could see the rows of fierce, bearded faces under spiked helmets lining their decks.

The leading ship, also the largest, had a kind of raised tower or castle near the stern. A giant banner displaying two crossed red axes against a black field flew from its timber battlements.

I saw a knot of Gothic officers standing under the banner. One of them, a towering figure in gleaming scale mail and a rich blue cloak, was Indulf, a former mercenary in the Roman army who had defected to the Goths. Totila had made him co-admiral of the fleet.

For all his talents, Totila was a poor judge of character. Indulf was a thief and a pirate, as well as a traitor, and his first instinct was to go for easy plunder instead of following orders.

John the Sanguinary's ploy had worked. Seeing the bait dangled before his eyes, Indulf had lunged at it like a starving dog, with no thought for the consequences, or the rest of the Roman fleet.

This was small comfort for us, who stood in his way.

"'Ware arrows!" bellowed the first mate. The Gothic archers packed onto the foredeck of the leading galley were bending their bows, aiming upwards to send their shafts sailing high across the water, down on our heads.

I crouched beside the mainmast, raising my pathetic little buckler for all the protection it offered. The thumping of the blasted drums was like thunder in my ears. I was consumed by terror, and struggled to retain control of my straining bladder.

The crew scattered under the lethal hail of arrows. One or two were unlucky. Shrieks of pain swept across the deck. My horses, still crammed into the hold below, heard the dreadful cries and responded in kind. The air filled with the noise of dying men and frightened animals, pounding drums, splashing oars, the zip and hiss of arrows, and the triumphant war-songs of the Goths.

"Shoot!" I heard our captain howl, "give the bastards some of their own gruel!" but resisted the urge to look up: every old soldier knows that is the surest way to receive an arrow in the eye.

The singing of the Goths rose to a great shout, and the rain of arrows ceased. Their flagship was slowly turning about to present her starboard flank to us, so her archers and javelin throwers could aim downwards and sweep our deck clean before boarding.

Seen close to, the enemy flagship was huge. Her maindeck loomed over us, packed with cheering warriors, working themselves up into a killing frenzy.

Four of our men lay scattered about the deck, twitching in their death-throes, bodies feathered with arrows. I observed the flights on the Gothic arrows were dyed red, the kind of irrelevant detail that men often notice in the heat of battle, as a distraction from impending death.

Another storm of arrows engulfed our ship, along with javelins and throwing darts. More screams. Three more of our men were ushered into death's embrace, and our captain's flow of orders were abruptly cut off.

I saw him clutching at an arrow in his throat, his face suffused with pain and rage. He staggered, trying manfully to pull the arrow free, lost his balance and toppled over the side. He vanished, though I heard a distant splash as his body crashed into the sea. Poseidon had claimed another victim.

Deprived of their leader, the crew's fragile discipline crumbled away. Some flung themselves into the sea after him, hurling away their weapons and leaping over the side. Others ran below to hide, or stood alone or in little groups, resolved to fight to the death.

Run or hide, stand or swim, death would come for them all. And me. I stood up, shivering and babbling prayers, and braced myself against the mast.

Our steersman had been killed, and no-one had replaced him at the tiller. The ship was starting to drift. Then the Goths hurled their grappling irons. The steel claws bit, and held fast, and our little helpless transport was dragged into the deadly embrace of their flagship.

Waves of Gothic warriors dropped aboard, howling like demons. They looked formidable enough, tall, long-haired men with shields and hatchets, their blue eyes flashing fire, but I had faced them before.

One of them spotted me and came bounding in for the kill. He was young, with just a downy scrap of beard on his chin, and eager to impress his comrades.

Too eager, and clumsy. His eyes were wild, and the veins pounded in the side of his neck. I advanced to meet him, planting my feet wide to guard against the pitch and roll of the ship.

His hatchet flashed through the air, aiming at my head. Once, I would have easily sidestepped the blow, but now was obliged to get my left arm up and deflect it with my buckler.

The shock of the impact sent jolts of pain coursing up my arm. I bit back a scream and stepped inside his guard, legionary-style, stabbing my sword at his exposed belly. Sharp steel ripped through the thin covering of his deerhide jerkin, up through his guts and into his heart.

I twisted out the blade, and his innards swiftly followed, a hot gush of wet, glistening, worm-like objects. He gurgled and crumpled into a heap, clutching feebly at the hole in his belly even as the fierce glow in his eyes faded and died.

Three of his comrades rushed at me, howling for vengeance. Even in my prime, I could not have fought so many, and chose the wiser part of valour. I turned and ran, or rather stumbled, tripping over a loose coil of rope and falling flat on my face.

I moaned in fear, rolling onto my side and expecting the steel kiss of a Gothic blade in my flesh. God saw fit to throw a Cilician in the path of my would-be killers, a huge man, naked save for a breechclout, wielding a cudgel with steel ingots hammered into its head.

He laid into the Goths with gusto while I crawled towards the hatch leading to the hold. My horses were still shrieking. A series of bangs and thumps from below told me that a few had broken loose from their pens. Rather than allow my stock to fall into barbarian hands, I intended to cut all their throats before doing the same to mine.

The strange duality between Elene's death, and the one I intended for myself, struck me as I reached for the ladder. She had ended her life in water, and now so would I. Perhaps our shades would meet in whatever afterlife was reserved for suicides – some dark corner of Hell, probably – and settle our differences at last.

The shrieks of dying men echoed inside my head as I crept down the rungs of the ladder, mingled with oaths and shouts and the ring of steel. Some of the crew had chosen to die hard and drag a few Goths into the afterlife with them.

I was nearly on the last rung before a great shadow blotted out the light streaming through the hatch above. For a second or two I was in total darkness, and then there was a shattering crash, the ship sagged violently to port, and I was hurled sideways off the ladder.

An ear-splitting animal scream tore through my skull as I landed heavily on the body of a fallen horse. She had broken loose from her pen, or been knocked out of it, and snapped a leg as she skidded wildly across the deck. For a moment we were tangled up together, a mutually terrified mess of flailing limbs and bodies, until I managed to roll clear.

"I'm sorry, I'm sorry," I found myself gasping, even though one of her hoofs had come within an inch of gelding me.

Her pain-filled eyes rolled wildly inside her beautiful sleek head, but I had no time for pity. Some gigantic missile had smashed a great hole in the foredeck, passed straight through the hull and the deck below, fatally holing the ship below the waterline.

Greenish seawater was now pouring in through the rent. The ominous creak of timbers placed under impossible strain echoed through the hold. Soon they would begin to snap and shatter, and the ship would split clean in half, spilling her contents into the deep.

I had to get out before she went down. Whimpering, I clawed my way back up the slanting deck.

My left arm was still numb from deflecting the hatchet, and felt like it might twist from the socket. Gasping with effort, black spots dancing before my eyes, I managed to curl my fingers round the side of the ladder.

The sound of cracking timber and rushing water filled me with dread. Pain screeched up the length of my arms as I grimly clung on, like a monkey dangling from a branch. The shuddering horse slid away from under me as the deck tipped again.

Now I was hanging almost vertically, with the world dropping away below me. Crates and barrels and struggling horses were pulled downwards into the insatiable maw of the sea.

Death beckoned. I fancied I could almost see his grinning spectre, crooking a bony finger at me.

"Not yet, you damned ghoul," I croaked, "go back to the pit!"

The spectre faded. Sheer desperation lent me the strength to drag myself up the ladder. Fires raged inside my ageing limbs, tendons and sinews stretched to their limits. The pain was unbearable. The alternative was death by drowning, the stuff of my nightmares.

Then the light was blotted out again. I fought my way upwards in pitch darkness, wincing as the crumbling ship was rocked by the impact of another shattering crash. Somehow she held together, but was sinking fast, dragged inexorably down by the sheer weight of water flooding her mangled hull.

I emerged from one kind of Hell, only to find myself in another. The maindeck rose above me like a timber wall, and then fell away again as the sea hurled the ship to starboard.

The planking was slick with blood and strewn with corpses and dying men. Their bodies rolled about the deck, but otherwise the ship was deserted. The few surviving crewmen had jumped overboard, while the Goths had fled back to their own vessel. There was no easy plunder to be had here, only death.

I heaved myself up the ladder and flopped onto deck. The bulk of the Gothic flagship still loomed to the west, and I could see its crew frantically sawing through the ropes of the grappling irons that still bound the two vessels together.

Another shadow flew over my head, like a great bird, briefly veiling the sun. This time it missed the transport and smashed into the hull of the Gothic ship, raising a great cloud of shattered timbers and a spray of blood.

It was no bird, but a load of rocks packed inside a net. The rocks broke and scattered on impact, shredding a number of luckless Gothic warriors and spreading fear and panic aboard the flagship. She already bore the scars of previous direct hits, including a jagged hole in her stern, just above the waterline.

I crawled, flat on my belly, over the main deck towards the starboard rail. There I saw the dark shapes of Roman warships, scudding through the sea like a pack of hunting sharks.

The largest of our galleys had catapults and ballistae mounted on their foredecks. Two of these stood a little way off, bombarding Indulf's ship with everything they had: rocks, flaming darts, baskets of burning coals.

In their haste to destroy the enemy flagship, the crews of the Roman war machines were none too accurate, and had accidentally hit the transport while I was climbing down into the hold.

The Gothic admiral had no such artillery, and was powerless to respond. All he could do was cut free of the sinking transport and try to escape before his vessel was smashed to pieces.

I had my own difficulties to contend with. Gulping with fear, I peered over the side and spotted some floating barrels and caskets, newly escaped from the hold. There was also a horse or two, forlornly trying to swim to safety. Their heads were just above water, but we were miles from land. Soon their strength would give out, and Poseidon would drag them under to join his feast of the drowned.

My fingers were numb with cold and fear as I wrenched at the laces of my helmet. I cast it away, and my sword-belt, and kicked off my boots.

"I cannot drown," I muttered, teeth chattering, "please God, do not let me drown."

The dying ship gave another unexpected lurch, and almost tipped me overboard as I climbed over the rail.

I looked down at the churning waters, closed my eyes, and with a final prayer let myself drop.

***

They fished me out after the battle was over, barely conscious and chilled to the bone. Two hours of floating in the sea, clinging to a wine barrel, does nothing for a man's constitution.

From this uncomfortable vantage point I had been able to witness the destruction of the Gothic fleet. Indulf's mindless greed proved the death of his cause. While his men plundered our transports and slaughtered the crews, the Roman warships to the north turned about and flew south to intercept him, driving a wedge between his squadron and the remainder of the Gothic fleet, led by a Goth named Gibal.

Our crews were more experienced than the Goths, and skilfully outmanoeuvred the lumbering enemy vessels, pounding them with artillery before closing to board. We also had more fighting men, and thinned out the numbers of Gothic warriors with showers of arrows and javelins. Rams were a thing of the past, so the issue was settled by exchanges of missiles and the murderous heat of close combat.

The above is a calm, concise overview of the sea-battle of Sena Gallica, such as might be taught in a schoolroom. At the time, clinging like a rat to my barrel, all I could see were the vast shapes of war galleys, Roman and Gothic, crashing together like sea-monsters.

My ears were full of water, but I could hear muffled noises of battle: men fighting and killing, screeching as they suffered mortal wounds and plunged into the sea, the endless thump-thump-thump of drums as the Gothic vessels floundered, oars flailing as they laboured to turn about. Their squadrons drifted and lost cohesion, allowing the faster, better-handled Roman ships to swoop in and pick off the stragglers.

The foaming seas were tainted with gore. I saw men drowning, stretching out their hands to me in futile supplication even as they went under. Limbs thrashing, blood spurting from terrible wounds and fouling the water. A few were lucky enough to catch hold of bits of wreckage, and bobbed about like human corks, tossed this way and that by the whim of the churning seas.

Our captains were thorough. Every time a Gothic ship was captured, the crew slaughtered or taken prisoner, it was set on fire and turned loose. Abandoned vessels drifted aimlessly about the sea, lit from stem to stern by raging fires.

The midday sun was hanging like a copper gong in the sky, partially obscured by leaping flames and clouds of smoke, when one of our dromons picked me up. It was trawling for Roman survivors in the water, and rowed close enough to hear my feeble gasps for help.

"Not dead yet, eh, grandfather?" remarked one of the grinning young sailors who threw me a rope and pulled me aboard. I would have collapsed on deck, but they caught me in their arms and gently lowered me onto my rump.

"Not dead yet," I agreed in a hoarse whisper. One of them passed me a bulging gourd of wine. I emptied it, glorying in the warmth spreading through my innards.

There were two or three others in the same condition. God, in his infinitely random mercy, had chosen to pluck us from the sea while our comrades drowned. We sat in miserable silence, wrapped up in layers of blankets and gnawing at the hard biscuits handed out by the crew.

The sailor who called me grandfather stood beside me, gazing at the aftermath of battle. I counted no less than thirty-six burning Gothic ships. A few were sinking, their gutted, charred carcases slowly dipping below the waves. The few survivors were in full flight, racing towards the distant port of Sena Gallica and safety, pursued by our triumphant fleet.

"Roma Victor," I heard the sailor whisper. A ragged cheer swept through the dromon, and then I fell asleep.

28.

Having smashed the Gothic blockade, our
fleet sailed on to relieve Ancona. We found
the garrison and the citizens on the verge of
starvation. It was a town populated by hollow-
cheeked ghosts, reminiscent of the pitiful
wretches I had seen wandering the baking
wastes of Perugia.

War brings nothing but famine and ruin and
misery to most, while any fleeting shreds of
glory are reserved for wealthy soldier-
aristocrats like John the Sanguinary. He, of
course, had won his great victory, and led his
guards through the streets in a tasteless
martial parade, banners flying and trumpets
blowing. Those few citizens who had the will
and the strength gathered on the pavement to
watch him pass. Mute, faded, scarecrow-like
figures, greeting his ridiculous procession in
baffled silence.

I went along to witness the farce, and could
not help but compare it to the triumph
awarded to Belisarius after his conquest of
North Africa: the entire populace of
Constantinople chanting his name as the
golden-armoured figure marched proudly
down the Mese at the head of his seven
thousand Veterans; the showers of golden
coins and medals he ordered to be distributed
from baskets to the mob; the Emperor

Justinian and his consort, robed in purple and gold and waiting to receive the victorious general in the Hippodrome.

By contrast, John was nothing, an ambitious courtier seeking to ape his betters, completely devoid of any self-awareness.

Nor, thankfully, was he aware of me. I kept to the shadows as he rode past on his high-stepping grey mare, hoping he thought me drowned.

Whether John had put me aboard one of the condemned transports out of personal spite, or on the orders of Narses, I could not be certain. Either one of those cold, calculating minds could have been responsible.

I was content to stay dead. The fleet was due to sail from Ancona up the coast to Ravenna, to wait for the arrival of the army led by Narses. I also wished to go to Ravenna, and there await my son, but not with the fleet.

All my horses were drowned, along with the majority of the transport crews. A horse-trader with no horses to trade is of little use, and I didn't care to let John know I was still alive. Instead I would travel to the capital by land, alone.

Some forty miles lay between Ancona and Ravenna. It was a risky journey. Rome still maintained some control over the eastern coast, but lacked the soldiers to send out regular patrols. I could well meet with a Gothic raiding party, who would either split my throat or let me go free, depending on their mood. They would never suspect that I was Coel ap Amhar ap Arthur, the British warrior in Roman service who once held the Sepulchre of Hadrian against their forebears.

First, I needed money. The sailors who rescued me from the sea had kindly given me a pair of old boots, a cloak, and enough wine and biscuit to sustain me for a couple of days. I had not a penny to my name, and so slept rough in an alley. Fortunately the late summer weather held, so the nights were warm, and the fleet departed for Ravenna on the morning of the third day after its victory over the Goths.

With John safely out of the way, I went in search of work. I eventually persuaded the landlord of a down-at-heel taverna down a narrow street in the poor quarter to hire me.

"The pay is shit, mind," he said, scratching his unshaven chin as he squinted at me, "you're a little old for a pot-boy, ain't you?"

"I'm clean, reliable and hard-working," I replied brusquely, "what more do you want?"

Nothing, was the answer, and so he set me to work. Picture, if you can, the one-time Roman general and owner of Caesar's sword, washing pots and serving foul ale and gruesome slop to a crowd of Italian drunks!

Come good fortune or bad, I have always made my way in this world. I slaved in the taverna for two months, renting a tiny garret in the cheapest hostel I could find in the poor quarter. What I lost in dignity I made up in coin, and by the end of that time had earned enough to buy a dagger and enough rations to last me to Ravenna.

I also hired a horse, a tough, wiry little hill pony from Campania, of the sort I wouldn't have allowed through the gates of my stables in Constantinople. She suited my purpose, though, and I paid the black-gummed ostler's outrageous price without quibbling. All I wanted was to get to Ravenna.

It was early November by the time I set out, a bad time for travelling, with icy winds sweeping in from the Adriatic and lashing the rocky coast. Careless of the weather, and the potential dangers of the road, I set out one blasted grey morning.

I neglected to inform the landlord of my departure. No doubt the greasy brute soon found another slave to wash his dishes and take his abuse.

The Flaminian road was largely deserted, and I passed just one convoy of wine-merchants taking their wares from Rimini to Ancona. Their heavily laden wagons were guarded by eight Sarmatian mercenaries. I remembered the Sarmatians who had escorted me and my mother to Constantinople: hard, brutal warriors from the broad steppes of Rus. They spared age nor sex during their bloodstained killing frenzies, and I took care to avoid their suspicious eyes.

Rimini, the scene of my bloodless victory over a decade previously, lay roughly midway between Ancona and Ravenna. The city was now again in Gothic hands. I was no longer in Roman service, and so planned to rest there for a night or two, safe behind its high walls, before continuing to Ravenna.

I spared my pony and led her on foot for most of the way, not wishing to exhaust her with the strain of carrying my bulk. Purple clouds were billowing across the sky by the time the distant lights of Rimini came in sight, a cluster of yellow pin-pricks against the gathering darkness to the north.

My soldier's instincts had grown rusty with disuse. The horsemen were on me almost before I saw them, grey shapes thundering out of a little cluster of woodland east of the road.

"Stay where you are," a man's voice shouted, "or you're dead."

I paused, one leg cocked over the pony's saddle. She wouldn't be able to carry me out of danger, not from these fleet riders.

"Steady," I whispered, stroking her neck as she whinnied and tossed her shaggy head in fear.

The horsemen clattered onto the road and spread out to surround me. I meekly folded my hands and waited, while making a swift inventory of their number and quality.

Eight men. Mounted on good horses, and with a military look and discipline about them. Each carried a long spear, a dagger, and was protected by a helmet and oval shield. Light cavalry, of the sort I had once led into battle.

"A first-rate ambush," I said when the dust had settled, "General Belisarius could have done no better. Though he practised his art against the enemies of Rome, not defenceless travellers."

One of the riders came forward. A tall, broad-shouldered man, with the look of a lancer about him. His face under the helmet was lined and grizzled, scorched by desert suns, and his eyes had a keen, knowing look.

"We are neither friends or enemies of Rome," he said, levelling his spear at my breast, "which are you?"

29.

I judged my answer carefully, with his spear-point hovering close to my heart.

"I am also for neither," I replied, "I am a deserter. Like you."

Those shrewd eyes narrowed, weighing me in the balance. Then he smiled and raised the spear.

"How did you know?" he asked, gesturing at his men to lower their weapons. He looked and sounded Germanic, though from which particular strand of that teeming people it was impossible to say.

"Old soldiers know deserters when they see them," I replied, "your men have good gear and horses, but have a slovenly, undisciplined look. You carry no flag and wear no insignia."

"We might be spies."

"You might. If so, you are in need of training. Spies should stick to their hiding places, instead of charging out like raw recruits to accost travellers."

I was forcing myself to speak boldly, gambling it would impress him. All the while, my innards were dissolving. Deserters or spies, these men were cut-throats, and would happily spill my blood if I uttered a word out of place.

One of the other riders trotted forward. "This is a waste of time," he snarled, "let's kill him and have done."

And be damned to you, I thought. "No," said the first man, who was clearly the leader of this troop of bandits, "he is a fellow spirit. Like us, he has deserted his flag and country, and taken to the road."

"What if he's lying? We can't afford to trust strangers."

My would-be killer was one of the ugliest men I had ever seen. His skin was raw and chapped, as though someone had poured boiling water on his face, possibly in an effort to improve it. Two deep-set little eyes, gleaming with malice, were set either side of a great curving dagger of a nose, under which resided a mean little mouth.

He was clearly itching to put his spear in me, and doubtless had the blood of many innocents on his hands. Such born killers have to be dealt with, and quickly.

His captain barked with laughter. "Trust?" he cried, "do I trust you, Gambara? Do I trust any of the Masterless Men? Not a bit of it. I sleep with one eye open, and one hand on my dagger."

The one named Gambara gave back, scowling, and his captain turned back to me. "I am Asbad," he said, "leader and master of this company of rogues. Give me your name and quality."

Asbad, I thought. A Gepid name. The Gepids were an Eastern Germanic tribe, and close kin to the Goths. In common with most German tribes, they were not particular in their loyalties, and happily enlisted under the banner of whoever paid them most.

"Coel ap Amhar ap Arthur," I replied promptly, "a Briton, recently in the service of Rome."

I thought it pointless to lie. Any brief fame I had enjoyed was long in the past. These men were all young, and would not have heard of me.

"A Briton, eh?" said Asbad, smoothing his greasy tunic, "and what are you doing on the Flaminian Way in time of war, alone, with nothing but that little knife to protect you?"

"I was heading to Ravenna to see my son. He lacks his father's wisdom, poor lad, and still follows the eagle."

Asbad smiled, and some of his men chuckled, which was pleasing to hear. With the exception of Gambara, I was winning them over.

"Your words have the ring of truth," said Asbad, "so you're either an honest man, or an accomplished liar. Either is welcome in the Masterless Men. How far can that pony carry you?"

I gave her muzzle a pat. "Far enough, though I would not like to push her. I am not as svelte as I once was."

"Good. No more than five or six miles of discomfort lies before her tonight. Mount, Coel ap Amhar ap Arthur. Your son will have to wait."

I knew better than to argue. Asbad's friendly tone could not conceal the true nature of the man. He was a wolf, and so were his followers. Italy was full of such roving bands, the inevitable debris of a long war. Some were ex-soldiers, others merely criminals, or natives who had lost their homes and families in the bloodshed and turned to highway robbery.

They robbed and murdered and plundered with impunity, living off the land and their fellow men, until justice caught up with them. Belisarius, who had a particular hatred of deserters, used to hang them by the dozen, and leave their bodies to swing by the roadside as a warning.

I climbed aboard my pony and followed Asbad and his Masterless Men into the trees. They had set up a temporary camp in the heart of the wood, but Asbad wanted to move on.

"Too close to Rimini," he explained, "and there has been little traffic on the road of late. Not worth the risk. We shall head inland."

We rode east, in the gathering gloom, following a rough track that wound out of the woods and over the rolling hill country beyond. Far ahead, stretching in a rugged line from north to south, lay the Appenines.

Even though I had fallen into the hands of thieves and cut-throats, I did not despair. I was alive, and unharmed, and Asbad appeared to have swallowed my tale of being a deserter. I suppose I was, in a way, though I had not enlisted in the Roman army. There had been enough truth in the lie to lend my words conviction.

Eight men was a small enough following. I entertained hopes of stealing a horse and slipping their grasp, when the time came, but these quickly turned to ash.

A few miles east of the Flaminian Way, we arrived at the gutted remains of a little village. It had been a peaceful place once, nestled in the crook of a fertile valley, until the Masterless Men descended from the hills with fire and sword. Most of the stone cottages were blackened wrecks. The maimed corpses of their inhabitants lay scattered about, but this was not the worst horror.

One of the cottages had been spared. There were men lounging outside it, eating a rough supper of bread and cheese. They rose to salute Asbad as we cantered down the single street, which ended in a basilica.

The basilica was the largest building in the village. It puzzled me why Asbad's men had not requisitioned it instead of one of the miserable little cottages. Though small, it was a pretty place made of pink stone, with a flat roof and a short flight of steps leading to an arched doorway.

"They tried to take refuge in there," said Asbad, grinning at me, "the women and children, I mean. And the priest."

I stared at him, and again at the mangled corpses. They were all men. Most had died fighting, or trying to, their fists still curled around rakes and pitchforks and other makeshift weapons.

The walls of the basilica were streaked with soot, spilling out from the narrow windows. Some dreadful urge made me dismount and walk slowly towards the steps.

"Only one door, see?" said Asbad, "they barred it from the inside. Stupid. No escape route. Every good soldier knows you always leave a means of escape."

I mounted the steps. The nailed and timbered door had been smashed in, and its edges were burned black. I stretched out my right hand and gave it a gentle push.

The people inside had been dead for several days. Little remained of them, save a few blackened cinders and bits of bone and hair. The flagstones of the long nave were tainted with grease, and the still air carried a vague hint of roasting meat.

I should have been sickened, but I had seen worse. Such things happened in war. With terrible clarity, I saw the last moments of the villagers trapped inside the basilica. Unable to get out, clutching each other in shrieking terror as the Masterless Men hurled flaming torches through the windows.

Stone doesn't burn, but flesh does. They had burned, these people, while their menfolk were slaughtered outside. I glanced at the charred remains of the altar, and imagined the priest, kneeling before it and muttering prayers even as the flames licked at his body.

I turned away, not wishing to dirty my already tarnished soul by looking too long.

Gambara was waiting for me at the foot of the steps. "Too strong for your stomach?" he asked, his little mouth curled into a grin, fists planted on his narrow hips.

"No," I replied, stepping closer, "how about yours?"

The ugly lines of his face wrinkled in confusion. He was a dull-witted sort, and failed to react in time as I seized the hilt of his dagger, drew it from the wooden sheath and rammed the blade into his gut.

His little eyes widened in shock. I left the dagger buried inside him, gripped his scrawny neck in both hands and threw him to the ground.

The back of his head cracked against the bottom step. Dark blood splattered the stone. I pulled him up and smashed his head against the step, again and again, with all the violence I could muster. His body jerked and went into spasm, blood and brains spilling from the shattered pulp of his skull.

Finally, when all the rage had gone out of me, I let the dead thing go and wiped my bloody hands on the grass.

Asbad and the rest of the Masterless Men had watched the killing in silence. Not one of them lifted a hand to help their comrade. Life was cheap among such people, and Gambara was not the sort to inspire affection.

I looked up, panting with exertion, at Asbad. He, if anyone, would have avenged the dead man.

"You can have his horse," he said, before turning away and calling for supper.

30.

I rode with the Masterless Men for months, all through the autumn and the long winter that followed. Asbad took a liking to me, while at the same time making it perfectly plain what would happen if I ever tried to leave his company.

"No-one leaves," he was fond of saying, "save in a box."

This was a favourite jest of his. A Masterless Man was lucky to be buried. If he fell sick, or was wounded in a skirmish, Asbad left him to rot. He judged men by their usefulness, and cheerfully tossed them aside if they showed signs of faltering.

"Scum," he termed us, "fit to adorn a gallows. Nothing more. I will lead you to profit or death, but don't expect mercy."

We were scavengers, feeding off the scraps of war. While Totila laid siege to the few remaining Roman garrisons in Italy, and Narses plodded around the Gulf of the Adriatic, the likes of the Masterless Men burned and pillaged and murdered as they pleased.

There was none to stop us. We had little to fear from the law, since neither the Goths or the Romans could spare the men to enforce it.

Occasionally the citizens of some particularly lawless province would band together to defend their homes. We might have easily scattered these hapless clods, with their cudgels and farm tools, but Asbad preferred to avoid conflict. He would never fight, unless we were starving or in dire need of shelter.

Under his bluff exterior beat the heart of a coward. I despised him, and all his followers, and wished I had the means to bring them all to justice. For months I witnessed them slaughter and rob and rape, bringing horrors I will not describe to isolated villages and farmsteads.

They thought me soft, for refusing to join in with the worst of their crimes. God forgive me, but I did nothing to stop them either. My quill falters as I think of the atrocities I witnessed.

Courage ebbs with age. If I had been a younger man, I might have chosen to die, sword in hand, defending the honour of some young girl the Masterless Men wished to brutalise. Instead I stood aside and prayed silently for death to come and take us all.

The wheel turned, and winter slowly melted into spring. During the worst of the cold months we sheltered in the foothills of the Appenines, inside a ruined tower Asbad claimed to be the palace of some long-dead king, but I reckoned was an old fortified byre for cattle.

One blustery evening in early April, as we sat huddled around a fire on the rough floor, Asbad's scouts returned with fresh tidings of the war.

"The Romans are on Italian soil," said one, a one-eyed Lombard ruffian named Agelmund, "we saw them marching down the coast to Ancona. Thousands of horse and foot. Too many to count."

"Thirty thousand," I muttered, and cursed as the bread I was toasting on the end of my sword dropped into the fire.

"I was in Constantinople when Narses was recruiting," I explained in response to all the hard looks, "the Emperor gave him all the money and men he desired. This is the largest Roman army to invade Italy for centuries."

"What of Totila?" demanded Asbad.

"He is at Rome, mustering all the men he can get," answered another of the scouts, "besides the people of his own race, he has hired a number of Lombards and Gepids."

"There are the imperial deserters, as well," said Asbad, "men Totila lured from their old allegiance with promises of easy plunder. What of you, Coel? Would you sell your sword to the Goths?"

I would rather fornicate with rabid dogs, was the truthful answer. "To anyone who can afford it," I replied carelessly, earning myself a laugh from the others and a comradely slap on the back. They thought I was a fine fellow, if inclined to be soft-hearted and easy on women, and referred to me as their little priest, since I refused to take part in rape and the pillaging of holy places.

Asbad had no reason to welcome the arrival of Narses. All was set for the contending armies to clash in an epic pitched battle, thus bringing the long war to a close and finally deciding the ownership of Italy. This was wretched news for the Masterless Men, who lived off the consequences of war, and relied on it continuing for many years yet.

He brooded for weeks in his lonely mountain stronghold, sending out regular bands of scouts to watch Totila at Rome and Narses at Ancona, and report on any movements. I waited, and bided my time, and prayed for Arthur's wellbeing.

"Please God," I murmured every night, out of earshot of my godless comrades, "let him be safe. Bring him through every trial without hurt. If he must fight, let him not be struck down. Spare him, O Lord, and take me instead. I am old, and ready to die."

It was high summer before Narses made his move. From Ancona he marched north to Ravenna, forcing a path through the mountains since the Goths had destroyed the old Roman bridge on the Flaminian road. At Ravenna he rested his army for nine days before setting out again.

"He's marching on Rome," reported Agelmund, "straight down the Flaminian Way. Totila has moved out of the city to confront him."

I would not have credited Narses with such boldness, but then the eunuch constantly surprised me. His conduct of the war to date had been firm and decisive, as though placing him in overall command had instilled some sense of duty in place of his usual scheming avarice. For once, Justinian had demonstrated shrewd judgment.

An idea came to me. "We should be present, when the armies meet," I said, "remain out of sight while the battle rages, and then descend on the field after all is over. Think of it! All those thousands of dead men. The plunder would be immense."

"Too risky," Asbad replied quickly, "what if we were spotted by outriders?"

I could almost smell his fear, and his followers looked unimpressed. A few had already started to cast sidelong looks at their chief. I was sometimes tempted to encourage their doubts with a carefully placed word here and there, but refrained, not wishing to put myself in danger. It is in the nature of thieves to fall out among themselves, and I predicted Asbad would suffer a fatal accident before the summer was out.

He sensed the disquiet of his men. After a bit more whining and protesting, he agreed to my plan by pretending it was his own.

"We shall track the line of march of the Romans," he said, "Totila will have to advance to meet them somewhere on the Flaminian road. Until the slaughter is over, we keep our distance."

"Then," he added, baring his brown teeth in a snarl, "the wolves shall descend."

31.

The Masterless Men rode out in force from their lonely hilltop fortress. There were twenty-seven in all, a disparate collection of Goths, Isaurians, Lombards, Gepids and I know not what else. And, of course, a single Briton.

Asbad sent two bands of scouts on ahead to discover the precise location of the contending armies. Agramond's men returned first. They found us picking our way through a ravine, surrounded by the frowning heights of the snow-capped Appenines.

"The Romans have taken up position over there," said Agramond, pointing his spear to the south, "on a plain near Taginae."

I could see nothing but mountains in that direction, but Asbad knew the country better. "Onward, then," he said, "but slowly."

He took us south via a difficult route, through a winding defile with sheer walls of rock rising either side of us. The way was so narrow in places we had to ride in single file, and Asbad insisted on absolute silence.

The ground sloped gradually upward. It was oppressively hot, and clouds of midges buzzed and danced around us, irritating the horses.

We emerged on a high ridge, overlooking a broad expanse of grassy plain. The plain was entirely ringed by mountains, a hollow crown of jagged white peaks, thrusting like colossal daggers into the peerless blue sky.

It was a glorious sight, and at another time I might have enjoyed the view. Instead my eye was drawn to the north-west, where Narses had drawn up his army.

I am a Briton at heart, of the old blood of British princes, but did not serve all those years in the Roman army for nothing. After the long, weary months of captivity, and the degrading company of thieves, the sight of the eagle stirred something dormant in my soul.

"He has arranged them well," I said, the first and only time I paid a compliment to Narses, "Belisarius could have done no better."

Narses had indeed done well. The little chess-master was something of a soldier after all, and possessed a martial spirit under the soft powdered flesh and opulent trappings of the courtier.

He had taken up a defensive position, securing what little high ground existed, on the north-west edge of the plain. A mile or so to his east was the little village of Taginae, which gave the region its name. The village was deserted, for the prudent inhabitants had fled into the mountains until all was quiet again.

In the centre of the Roman army, massed in a single dense phalanx of infantry, were the foederati troops, Huns and Heruls and

Lombards and the levies from Thrace and Illyria. They numbered some ten to fifteen thousand men, presenting a long, unbreakable wall of shields.

My spirits rose at the sight of the forest of banners and streamers, garishly painted with the crude symbols of the various tribes in Roman service: the wolf and the fox, stag's heads with spreading antlers, swooping hawks and snarling bears.

On the flanks of the infantry, protected by lines of stakes and hastily-dug ditches, Narses had placed his archers. Isaurians mostly, mixed with a few Sassanids and Thracian slingers. The Roman battle-line resembled a crescent, with the archers on the wings inclining slightly towards the infantry in the centre.

"It's a trap," said Asbad, who had also been studying the Roman formation, "if the Goths attack the Romans in the centre, they will be shot to bits by the archers on the flanks. This Narses is a shrewd devil."

I agreed, and smiled as I imagined the eunuch sitting in his pavilion, thoughtfully planning the deployment of his army with chess pieces representing the various units.

My heart clenched as I saw what lay in wait behind the archers. Narses had also stationed his cavalry on the wings, squadrons of lancers and horse-archers, including the elite bucelarii. Somewhere among them, assuming he had survived the long march from Salona, was my son.

It was agonising, knowing he was so close, but unable to go to him. "Stay where you are, old man," snapped Asbad, noting my anxiety, "dare to give away our position, and I'll put my sword through your heart."

My contempt for Asbad instantly soured to hatred, and I swore a silent oath he would not live out the day. I am in the habit of keeping my oaths.

For long hours we waited, listening to the distant throb of drums. Narses kept his men in position, but allowed them to rest and eat their rations, so they would be in prime fettle when the Goths appeared.

Asbad grew increasingly impatient. "Where in Hades are our scouts?" he fumed, "for that matter, where is Totila? Has the famed warrior king turned craven at last, and chosen to hide behind the walls of Rome?"

We didn't know it then, but his second band of scouts had been caught and massacred by a troop of Gothic outriders. Their bodies lay cooling a few miles to the south, a fitting end for such villains.

The noonday sun was just starting to dip when Totila finally arrived. His vanguard poured through the mountain passes from the south, thousands of lancers in shining mail, followed by disciplined squadrons of infantry. The Gothic spearmen wore no mail but relied on the protection of large, rectangular wooden shields, with archers and slingers on their flanks.

Totila had mustered all the troops he could in haste, but it soon became clear he was outnumbered. I expected his cavalry to deploy on the flanks of his army, but instead five hundred lancers of the vanguard clapped in their spurs and charged straight at the Romans.

It was insane, the most desperate gamble I had ever witnessed on a battlefield. "What are they doing?" I exclaimed, "five hundred men against thirty thousand? They will be slaughtered."

"Good," remarked Asbad, rubbing his hands, "let the killing began. The horses those lancers ride are worth a small fortune."

I thought a Gothic captain had chosen to disobey orders and launch a wild, suicidal charge against the Romans. In reality they were acting on the orders of their king.

On the left of the Roman position was a small hill, guarded by a detachment of spearmen. If the Goths could seize the hill and hold it, they would be able to turn the Roman flank.

The lancers swung to the right, galloping out of range of the Roman archers, and charged up the flanks of the hill. Even on our lofty height we could hear their war-cries, and the ominous thunder of hoofs as they surged in for the kill.

"Hold!" I shouted, gripping my reins until my knuckles turned white, willing the little band of spearmen to close up and repel the Gothic onslaught. They were Isaurians, the toughest infantry in Roman service, a stubborn race of peasants and hill farmers. I remembered the Isaurians I once led, and how I had cursed and flogged them before they showed me a little grudging respect.

Such men do not break, not easily. Their shield-wall vanished under the impetus of the Gothic charge, and for a moment all was waving banners and stabbing spears and flashing blades, rising and falling amid a sea of bodies.

A trumpet sounded, somewhere to the north, cutting through the din of battle. On the summit of the hill, above the heaving throng, I glimpsed a lone horseman.

My heart died inside me, and rose again from the ashes. The horseman was Arthur. It was impossible to see his face from such a distance, but his sword flamed into being when he ripped it from the scabbard. Caesar's sword, burning like a silver candle in his grip: Caledfwlch, the Hard Hitter, the Red Death, the Flame of the West.

I yelled in wordless, spluttering excitement, fairly bouncing up and down in my saddle, and drawing baffled glances from the

Masterless Men. A few of them already thought I was touched in the head, and this only confirmed it.

A line of riders appeared at Arthur's side. Heruls, his men, light horse armed with spears and shields. They couldn't stand against heavy Gothic lancers in a straight fight, but Arthur was a born soldier, with the blood of warrior princes coursing through his veins. He led them down the hill in a lance-shaped formation, with himself as the tip, aiming for the exposed enemy flank.

The Gothic charge had foundered on the Isaurian shields. They rode in baffled circles around the stubborn ring of spears, hurling axes and broken lances at Isaurian faces in an effort to smash gaps in the line.

Arthur chose his moment to perfection. He and his men plunged into the Goths like a blade into exposed flesh. In a second the Gothic lancers were reduced to a struggling mass of rearing beasts and panicking men, spilling back down the hill in hopeless confusion. Arthur's riders made dog meat of them, slashing riders from their saddles left and right, while the Isaurian spearmen broke formation and joined in the slaughter, dragging down and butchering as many Goths as they could catch.

I could not restrain a whoop of joy as the Goths fled in total disorder back to their own lines. Sensibly, Arthur did not pursue, but wheeled his men about and led them back to the hill, with the blood-sated Isaurians jogging in pursuit.

"That your boy, was it?" asked Asbad, who had watched the brief fight in silence, "he's quite the cavalryman. I never saw better. Sure his mother wasn't a horse?"

He grinned, and a few of his men snickered. I bit my tongue, wincing as I drew blood, and repelled the urge to draw my sword and chop his craven head off. My time would come.

Having failed in his bold effort to seize the hill, Totila resorted to delaying tactics. His army, when fully deployed across the southern expanse of the plain, was barely two-thirds the size of the Roman host. More Goths were marching up from the Flaminian road, and Totila needed to delay the battle until they arrived to bolster his slender lines.

First he tried negotiation, sending envoys under a flag of truce to drip lying offers of peace into Narses' ear. The eunuch scornfully rejected them all, but made his own offer in return, claiming he would spare the lives of Totila's warriors if the King surrendered and delivered himself up as a captive. Totila, unsurprisingly, failed to respond.

He switched tactics, sending the pick of his warriors into the space between the armies to make challenges of single combat. Some of these were accepted, and the Masterless Men amused themselves by laying bets on the winners.

I vividly recall one such duel. Totila sent out a truly gigantic warrior, one of the biggest men I ever saw, and this giant rode back forth before the Roman lines, bellowing out his challenge.

For a long while none cared to step forward and accept. He spat in contempt of Roman cowardice, and was about to turn his horse, when an officer broke away from Narses' bodyguard and galloped into the open.

I could not see the officer clearly – they were tiny, doll-like figures at this distance – but he was dwarfed by his opponent.

"Four siliqua on the giant," offered the man next to me, producing a handful of silver coin and weighing it in his hand.

"Done," I said, and we shook hands. It may seem a foolish wager, but size is not all. I didn't have the money anyway.

The two warriors rode to midway between the armies, and there faced each other. Cheers and shouts burst from Roman and Gothic throats as they clapped in their spurs and charged together.

At the last moment, the Roman officer swerved sideways, avoiding the other's lance, and rammed his spear under the giant's ribs.

It ran clean through that enormous body and burst out of his spine. The Goth stiffened in the saddle, and for a few seconds kept his seat as his horse slowed to a canter. Then, to catcalls from the Romans and groans from the Goths, he slowly toppled over and collapsed to earth like a falling tree.

"Four siliqua," I said, grinning as my beaten opponent threw his money at my face.

Still the Gothic reinforcements had not arrived. Narses might have advanced against the inferior numbers of the enemy, but he lacked the dash and fire of Belisarius.

"In chess," I could hear his piping voice in my head, "one does not simply throw all one's pieces forward in an all-out assault."

Totila resorted to an extraordinary piece of theatre. He rode out alone from his army, clad from head to toe in golden armour that outshone the sun, and mounted on a huge white stallion. Bound to his shoulders was a cloak made of some rich purple stuff. It streamed behind him as he cantered towards our infantry.

A kind of awed silence fell across the Masterless Men. I had no reason to love Totila, but was struck dumb by his valour. It was like something from Greek legend – a king in golden armour, riding forth to attack an enemy host single-handed.

The King of the Goths had no intention of throwing away his life. When he came to the midway point, near where his giant was struck down, he suddenly reined in his stallion.

He uttered a piercing cry of defiance and tossed his lance high into the air. Then he caught it, whirled it above his head, and started to make his horse prance in circles, as I had seen performers do in the Hippodrome.

"Is he a king, or a circus act?" growled Asbad.

It didn't end there. Mocking applause broke from the Roman ranks as Totila continued to toss and catch his spear, throw himself backwards in the saddle before suddenly regaining his seat, and make his horse spin and dance.

He performed for the best part of an hour, an impressive feat for a man covered in armour. When he was done, he gave a last shrill cry and spurred his sweating horse back to the Gothic lines, to a storm of cheers from his adoring troops.

I heard later, from one of Narses' bodyguards, that the eunuch made the following remark:

"Very impressive. Is it my turn now?"

His officers laughed, but Totila had succeeded in delaying the battle. His long-awaited two thousand auxiliaries had finally emerged from the mountains, somewhat disordered from their forced march, and joined his infantry in the centre.

The Goths were still in a grim position. To me, it seemed obvious Totila had to withdraw. He could have holed up behind the walls of

Rome, as Belisarius did when confronted with overwhelming numbers, and dared Narses to prise him out.

The Goths, however, only respected a monarch who displayed strength and daring on the battlefield. A tactical retreat was not in their belligerent nature. Like the Vandals, they remained to the last a warlike people.

Totila willingly embraced his doom. He ordered his cavalry forward, eight thousand or so lancers with horse-archers on the flanks, and formed them into five big squadrons. It was an awesome sight, hundreds of steel riders forming into lines across the plain, banners flapping overhead.

In a vain bid to intimidate the Romans, Totila had his infantry yell war-songs and beat incessantly on their drums.

"Noise won't break the Roman wall," I said confidently, "and nor will those horsemen. Run away, you foolish barbarians! You don't stand a chance."

The cavalry started to move, rolling forward at a slow trot. Totila had put himself in the central squadron. His royal standard, displaying two crossed golden axes against a red field, was clearly visible. He had put off his golden ceremonial armour for a standard helmet and cuirasse, but wore royal robes of purple and gold, and a scarf embroidered with precious stones wound about his neck.

Faster, faster, the tide of steel and horseflesh moved, shifting into a trot, a canter, and then a full-blown gallop. This was warfare as the poets understood it, a glorious last-ditch charge against the odds, brothers in arms, sweeping forward across a fair plain to conquer or die.

Sadly for the Goths, they were up against Narses, who possessed not an ounce of poetry or romance in his corrupt little soul. Safe behind a triple line of bodyguards, he sat on a chair mounted on a cart (he was unable to see over their heads otherwise) and calmly watched his enemies ride into the trap.

"Now," I murmured when I judged the Goths were within range of our archers.

The summer sky was briefly darkened by a storm of arrows. I saw the front ranks of the Gothic cavalry founder, horses and men tumbling to earth, but the rest came on, galloping straight over the bodies of their comrades.

It was impossible not to admire their courage. The horse-archers were destroyed in moments, melting away under the relentless hail of arrows. The few survivors wheeled their ponies and fled, leaving hundreds dead and dying behind them and spreading a tremor of panic through the watching Gothic infantry.

The lancers thundered into the Roman infantry. I chewed my lip as our shield-wall buckled and retreated a few steps under the impact of that wild charge, but the Goths lacked the weight of numbers to break it.

A peal of trumpets rang across the field. Reserves of footmen were sent in to bolster our sagging line, while the archers poured forward to shoot into the flanks of the struggling Goths.

Narses was conducting the battle with calm skill. He had carefully planned his strategy and predicted the moves of his opponent, who was a brave man and an inspirational leader, but no great tactician.

The Goths fought with the unyielding courage of men who expected to die. Their flanks were swiftly shot to pieces, and they could make no headway against the wall of shields, but still they fought on. Time and again they rallied around their standards, swinging swords and axes until every man was shot or speared from the saddle. Their blood-slathered corpses lay in heaps, the flower of a nation's fighting men, slaughtered by their own brave folly.

"Senseless massacre," remarked Asbad, "Totila is not fit to command. A good leader leads his men to profit, not death."

"Or glory," said Agremond, who had no love for his chief. His hand moved slightly towards his dagger. I tensed, waiting for him to make his bid for the leadership of the Masterless Men. If he drew steel on Asbad, I was fairly certain others would follow.

Agremond's nerve failed him at the crucial moment. Frustrated, I turned my attention back to the battle.

The Gothic squadrons were broken up, shattered beyond repair, over half their number lying stretched on the bloodied grass. A few hundred men, the best of them, fought on doggedly in isolated groups. Eighty or so formed up around the royal banner, resolved to defend it, and their king, to the last.

Asbad craned his neck, his eyes narrowing as they searched the field. "There," he said, pointing at the distant figure of Totila, fighting like a madman alongside his remaining bodyguards, "keep him in your sight."

The courage of most men has its limits. A few of the Goths wheeled their horses and fled, galloping back the way they had come, over ground liberally scattered with dead and dying.

This was enough to break the wavering spirit of the Gothic infantry, who had done nothing but stand and watch the methodical destruction of their comrades. The ordered lines of spearmen and archers rapidly disintegrated into a mob of fugitives, casting aside their weapons and streaming south towards the Flaminian road. I had seen a rout before, even participated in a few, and recognised the all-consuming terror that drives trained soldiers to panic and run for their lives.

Asbad had no interest in the fate of the infantry, though their discarded gear was of some value. He kept his eyes fixed on the carnage to the north, where the last of Totila's warriors were being overwhelmed and cut down.

"There!" he shouted, jabbing his finger at the royal standard, "there is our quarry!"

The standard was moving away from the battlefield, while Totila's few surviving guards dragged their master out of the fighting and threw him across a horse. He was badly wounded, one hand clutched to his bleeding side, and in no condition to prevent them leading him away. Otherwise he would have happily stayed to meet his end on Roman blades.

I thought Asbad fixated on mere plunder, but he had it in mind to slay a king. "Forward, if you wish to be rich men!" he shouted, clapping in his spurs and urging his horse down the rocky slope.

Seeing his intention, the Masterless Men gave a great shout and spurred after him. I followed, grateful for the opportunity to get closer to the battle – and Arthur – and to put an end to Asbad.

The Gothic army was in full flight, thousands of fleeing horse and foot scattered across the plain. Asbad and his men galloped through them, riding over those who failed to get out of the way in time, hacking down the few who showed fight.

I made no attempt to strike at the fugitives. There was only one man I wanted to kill that day, and I kept my eyes fixed on his back.

The Masterless Men intercepted Totila and his guards on the western edge of the plain. Only five men remained to the wounded king, but these five prepared to sell their lives dearly, forming a protective circle around him.

Asbad hung back while his followers tore into the hopelessly outnumbered guards. The skirmish was brief and bitter, and nine Masterless Men died before the five were slain.

They died well, those men, and their bloody-handed killers honoured them by immediately plundering the corpses. The thieves growled and snapped at each other, fighting for the possession of rings ripped or cut from dead fingers.

Seeing Totila alone and defenceless, Asbad struck. He charged in, spear levelled, and impaled the king's body, through the gap between the dented plates of his cuirass.

Totila slumped over his horse's neck, coughing blood, while Asbad wheeled away in triumph.

"I killed the king!" he shouted excitedly, "I killed the king!"

His celebration was short-lived. I galloped in behind him, judging my aim carefully, and unleashed a scything cut at his neck.

It was a sweet blow. My sword was an ugly, ill-balanced thing, but with a finely honed edge. It cleaved smoothly through the back of Asbad's thick neck and neatly sliced off his head.

The head span away, eyes glazing, mouth still stretched in a frozen grin. I saw it land and bounce a couple of times, before a fleeing horse trod on it. The skull burst like a rotten melon, scattering what passed for Asbad's brains all over the trampled earth.

None of the Masterless Men made any effort to avenge their chief. They were distracted by plunder, and three of the most avaricious, including Agramond, were already tearing at the body of Totila. They fought over his rich vestments, spattered with blood and mire, and Agramond dragged the jewel-encrusted scarf from his neck.

He would have made off with it, but one of his comrades struck at him with a sword, cutting off his left arm at the elbow. The bloodied scarf fluttered to earth, along with Agramond's severed limb. I was minded to leave the thieves to their work, but then we were overrun by a tide of yelling horsemen.

They were Huns, despatched by Narses to capture Totila and bring him back alive as a valuable prisoner. Furious at seeing him dead, they set about butchering his killers.

Outnumbered and outmatched, the Masterless Men were slaughtered. I clung to my horse's right side, determined not to raise my head, and was swept away in the swirling mass of fighting men and screaming horses.

"Kill these pigs! Just kill them!" someone howled, and I saw a Roman officer cut with his spatha at a robber's face. The heavy chopping edge sliced away the top of his victim's head, leaving only the lower part of the jaw intact.

The officer wore lamellar armour over his chest and thighs, liberally stained with blood, and had lost his crested helmet in the fighting. I would have recognised his lean, greying, sharp-nosed face anywhere this side of Hell.

"Bessas!" I shouted, my voice cracking as I tried to make myself heard, "Bessas – it's me, Coel! Roma Victor!"

Bessas reined in, blood dripping from his sword, and looked around. He was never one for smiling, but I thought the corners of his sour little mouth hitched up a little when he spotted me.

"So it is," he said, as though my presence was nothing remarkable, "and after all this time you still neglect to salute a superior officer!"

32.

Bessas was in command of the Huns, and managed to restrain them from killing me. Instead they sated their bloodlust on my erstwhile comrades.

I had spent many months in the company of the Masterless Men, but cannot honestly pretend I felt a shred of pity for them. They were criminals of the lowest stamp, thieves and murderers and rapists, and rode with Death constantly grinning at their shoulders. At Taginae, his skeletal hands gathered them up.

When all was over, and the Huns had gathered up the body of Totila, Bessas escorted me to the Roman lines. Dusk was falling as we picked our way over the wreckage of the Gothic army. Weary but victorious Roman soldiers were moving among the piles of bodies, looking for fallen comrades and finishing off wounded Goths.

"A familiar reek," he remarked, lifting his long snout to sniff the rank air, "blood and death and terror. You and I have sampled it on a fair few battlefields, eh?"

I was in no mood to reminisce about past campaigns. "Bessas," I said anxiously, "what do you know of my son? Did he survive the battle?"

"Never fear. Arthur came through it without a scratch, and distinguished himself into the bargain. Did you see him repel that first Gothic charge? I found myself wondering who his real father was."

He spoke in jest, and I was relieved enough to laugh with him.

We reached the northern edge of the battlefield, where the Gothic cavalry had broken their teeth on the Roman shields. The Roman infantrymen had broken up into their respective tribes, and something like a festival atmosphere had settled over the army. Men laughed and joked around their campfires, their good humour fuelled by the barrels of ale and mead and wine Narses had supplied them.

There was a slightly hysterical edge to their laughter. These men were the ones who had survived, and come through the battle unscathed. If you listened hard, you could hear the distant screams of their wounded and dying comrades in the medical tents, where our surgeons were practising their art.

I noticed Bessas was taking me to the grand central pavilion, where the banner of the eagle flew in triumph.

"I have no wish to see Narses," I said, halting, "he thinks I'm dead. Let him."

"You could not hope to deceive him for long," replied Bessas in his matter-of-fact way, "and you must come, if you wish to see your son. Arthur is in the general's pavilion.

Narses has invited him to dinner, along with any other officers who distinguished themselves today."

I might have feared a trap, but this was Bessas, one of the most honest men in the Roman army, even if that wasn't saying much. With a sigh, I followed him to the pavilion.

Narses was still guarded by his toy soldiers, richly-armoured gallants with crests on their silver helmets. I responded to their stares with a sneer and a rude gesture, and laughed when one reached for his sword.

"Careful," I said, "the rust might make the blade stick."

He went red, but Bessas caught my arm and led me inside before any further pleasantries could be exchanged.

The interior was just as tastelessly opulent as I remembered from my last meeting with Narses at Ancona. Added to the rich carpets and stench of incense was the warbling of a young male singer in the corner, accompanied by a girl plucking on a lyre. They looked like siblings, with the same angelic faces and crisp blonde hair, and were probably slaves, bought by Narses at great expense from the market in Constantinople.

Their gentle music was all but drowned by the coarse laughter of soldiers, sitting or sprawling on a number of divans arranged in a rough circle in the middle of the pavilion. The wine was flowing, and had been for some time judging by the drunken conversation and coarse jests flying about.

Narses was lounging on the smallest of the divans, wearing a plain white robe with a silver circlet on his brow. His friend, John the Sanguinary, sat at his right hand, dressed in a manner which might have been considered extravagant by an opium-addled Persian whoremaster. He was a vision in rich silks of many hues, green and gold and crimson and God knows what else. Pale gold rings flashed on his fingers of his right hand as he delicately stifled a yawn. No mean soldier himself, the company of soldiers evidently bored him.

I cared nothing for either of them, and looked eagerly among the crowd of red faces for my son.

Arthur had already spotted me. He rose from his divan and strode across the floor to embrace me, his face glowing with wine and joy.

"Father!" he shouted, "is it really you?"

Unlike most of the others, he still wore his armour, and Caledfwlch was bound to his hip. I submitted to his crushing embrace, wincing as I felt my ribs creak, while he roared and pounded me on the back.

The Bear of Britain, they used to call my grandsire, or so my mother told me. Arthur senior had been a big, fearsomely strong man, and his descendent was no weakling. I was glad of that, but also needed to breathe.

"Loosen your grip a little," I wheezed, "else my lungs will pop."

He subsided, still laughing, and held me at arm's length. His green eyes sparkled, and for a moment I fancied his mother was looking at me through them.

"They said you were dead," he said, giving me a shake, "drowned off the coast of Sena Gallica. God's bones, how I wept for you! Where have you been all this time?"

His bull-horn of a voice rang in the silence. The din of music and conversation had died away, and over Arthur's shoulder I saw Narses watching me with a cold glitter in his eyes.

"I see a ghost has come to join our little celebration," said the eunuch, "one I thought laid to rest at the bottom of the ocean, many months ago."

I gently pushed Arthur aside. "I am no ghost," I replied, "but solid flesh and bone. Bessas, prove it."

Bessas gave one of his rare grins and punched me on the arm.

"Coel is alive," he declared, "if a trifle bruised."

Narses steepled his fingers and glanced sidelong at John, who was glaring at me with an expression I can only describe as two parts disbelief to one part sheer hatred.

"Well, well," said Narses, "perhaps you walked ashore across the seabed. You are a hard man to kill. No wonder Britain proved so difficult to conquer, if all the natives are like you."

"You admit it, then," I said accusingly, "you admit deliberately plotting my death at Sena Gallica, by placing me aboard one of the condemned transports."

Narses gave a little shrug. "Not at all. I bear you no particular ill-will, though you have proved relentlessly stubborn in your refusal to serve me. It was John who tried to kill you at Sena Gallica. If you had been in my employ then, I would not have allowed it."

John's handsome head snapped around, and he glared venomously at his friend. "Damn you!" he hissed, "you dare accuse me of such a thing, in public, in front of fellow officers?"

"I accuse you of nothing," Narses replied, unmoved, "I state it. I am in command here. Everyone present would do well to remember that simple truth."

He inclined his oversized head to his left, to a man who looked like a high-ranking barbarian, with long yellow hair and drooping moustaches. His intelligent blue eyes studied me carefully, and Arthur, and occasionally dropped to look greedily at Caledfwlch.

"This is Pharamond," said Narses, "an envoy from Theodobald, King of the Franks. He is our honoured guest."

I failed to see the envoy's relevance, but Narses never said or did anything without a carefully planned reason.

"Theodobald is a young man," he prattled on, "a very young man indeed, just sixteen years old, and new to power. I am glad to say he is a sensible youth, and wishes to be a friend to Rome. Hence the presence of Pharamond, who witnessed our victory today."

"The young king seeks to learn wisdom from history. He has read of the exploits of his warlike forebears, and eagerly devours the legends and chronicles of other nations. Including those of your own fair isle, Coel."

I kept a careful eye on Pharamond while Narses talked. The envoy had a lean and wolfish look about him, and kept toying with the hilt of his sword.

"Your return was an unlooked-for gift from God," Narses continued, "I see that now. Theodobald is gathering not only wisdom, but all the relics of the ancient world he can find. Relics, as everyone knows, hold power."

"The sword," growled Pharamond, "the sword that belonged to Caesar, and was forged by the gods. Give it to us."

I looked to Arthur, whose face had darkened with anger. "What is this?" he cried, clapping his hand to Caledfwlch, "you mean to give my inheritance to some barbarian chieftain? Not while I live!"

"Nor me," I said, moving to stand beside him. "Caesar's sword belongs to our family."

I looked to Bessas, but the veteran stood silent, frowning into his grey beard. He had always lacked for resolution, and was one of those who failed to support Belisarius when the general needed him at Ravenna.

The other officers were all young men, bold and valiant in their way, but hopelessly drunk, and unable to comprehend what was happening. Narses held us all in the bowl of his hand.

"Caesar's sword is the property of the Empire," Narses squeaked, "as the Emperor's chief representative in Italy, it is mine to dispose of as I see fit. King Theobald has heard the stories of your famous ancestor, Coel, and wants his magic sword. He thinks it will bring him good fortune in war."

His eyes narrowed to slits. "It is also the price Theobald demands for not supporting the Goths in this war. They are all kin, these barbarians. Unless we give him the sword, he will lead a hundred thousand warriors over the Alps into Roman territory. There will be no famine to stop them this time."

"Come," he added, spreading his hands, "it is only an old sword, after all. Place it on the carpet at Pharamond's feet, and let us all be friends."

I became aware of the presence of armed men at my back. Narses' guards had shuffled into the pavilion. At least one of them, I knew, would relish the chance to stick his sword in my liver.

A tense silence filled the silken chamber. Narses sat upright, his short legs dangling over the edge of his divan. Beside him, John looked distrustfully at everyone, long fingers curled about the jewelled hilt of his dagger. Pharamond glared at me and my son, willing us to give up our rightful property.

I turned my head slightly to the left. "Beware of rust," I whispered, and ripped out my sword.

Arthur threw himself aside in time, else I might have taken his head off. I struck blind, knowing there were at least two men behind me. The blade smacked against a silver helmet, severing a cheek-guard and knocking its owner to the floor.

The sound of clashing steel jerked Bessas to life. He threw himself at one of the guards, and they went down in a roaring, cursing heap, scrabbling for their daggers.

"Stop this madness!" shrieked Narses, his voice resembling a kettle coming to the boil, "guards! Guards – someone turn out the guard!"

Most of his guests remained where they were, frozen in shock, but one or two saw an opportunity to win their general's favour. They struggled to their feet, looking around blearily for their swords, only to have Arthur descend on them like a raging giant.

His fists smashed them to the floor, and then John flew at him, curved dagger raised to strike. Arthur blocked the strike with his forearm, kneed John in the crotch and threw him bodily across the pavilion. The screeching nobleman crashed into Narses' divan, overturning it and sending the eunuch flying.

He landed heavily against the pillar carrying the bust of the Emperor Elagabalus. The bust toppled from its perch and landed next to Narses, who lay stunned, staring into the late emperor's marble eyes in dumb confusion.

"Run!" shouted Bessas, who had got on top of his opponent, "run, you fools!"

I beckoned at Arthur, and together we ducked out of the pavilion into the night. Four more of Narses' guards were running towards us, drawn by the noise.

"Get those horses," rasped Arthur, pointing to a pair of beasts tethered to a tree beside the pavilion. They were being tended by a small, fair-haired servant boy, and probably belonged to Pharamond.

He bounded towards the guards, Caledfwlch whirling in his hand. The sword was like an extension of himself, and I could only watch in admiration as he made short work of the four men, killing one and severely wounding two. The last wisely took to his heels, howling for aid.

I had the easier task of dealing with the boy, who required only a sharp word and a cuff round the ear before he yelped and ran off into the darkness.

My fingers shook as I fumbled to untie the reins. I picked out the smaller of the horses for myself, a roan mare, and handed Arthur the sleek black stallion.

"He will better carry your weight," I said, throwing him the reins. He nodded and leaped into the saddle, while I scrambled aboard the mare with distinctly less grace.

Oaths and shouts came from the pavilion, mixed with the sound of fighting, as we steered our stolen horses to the north and heeled them into a gallop. None tried to stop us. Arthur was popular among the soldiers, and in place of a hail of arrows we were sent on our way by laughter and encouraging shouts.

They were the last Roman voices I ever heard.

33.

Just a little longer, and I reach the end of my tale. The mere effort of writing and remembering has drained the last of my strength.

Abbot Gildas, poor man, has watched me slowly fade away these past two years, since I first took up my pen. Only his respect for my age, and the knowledge that it would strip me of purpose in life, prevents him from forbidding me to write.

I began this, my last despatch, with an account of how I lost my son. It ended with me lying half-dead near the banks of the Po, bleeding my life out from a host of wounds.

The Frankish soldiers left me there to die. I was no value to them. They had pursued us all the way from the Roman camp at Taginae, to seize Caledfwlch and deliver it to their avaricious young king. If that meant killing me, and Arthur, then so be it.

I would have crawled to my horse, but the Franks had taken her. In any case, I could not ride, or even stand. My injuries were too great. As I lay in the mud, weeping in pain, I knew I would never be whole again.

All my concern was for Arthur. I last saw him riding west, towards the border of Liguria. The Franks would give chase, but he was a better rider than the lot of them, and had a fine horse.

I had no means of knowing his fate. All I could do was lie there, a used-up wreck, and wait for the spectre of death. All my contempt for Narses and his crippled state came back to haunt me. I was the cripple now, alone and friendless, and destined for a miserable end.

God was not quite done with me. Somehow I lasted the night, and in the morning an unwanted saviour came in the form of a Perugian priest. Like the Samaritan, he knelt by my side, whispered soothing words, and did his best to bind up the worst of my wounds.

"Leave me, father," I begged, but he would have none of it. He was an old man, lacking the strength to help me stand, so he went and fetched a couple of farm boys from the nearest village. They brought a cart, drawn by an ox, and lifted me aboard under the priest's careful supervision.

For weeks I lingered, hovering between life and death in the back room of a farmer's cottage. He resented my presence, and the duty of caring for me, but the old priest's word was law in the village.

"You are not well, my friend," my saviour said to me one chill winter's morning, "we have done our poor best, but your leg…God denies us the skill to heal you entire."

He was lonely in his little church, and wished me to remain as his assistant. I had no intention of ending my days as the lackey to some village priest, no matter how kind.

My left leg was badly twisted, but I could limp well enough with the aid of a stick. One moonless night, while the farmer was lying abed, swine drunk and shaking the rafters with his snoring, I crept into the stable and took his horse.

I had not ridden for weeks, and the horse was a fat old mare, ruined by years of heaving ploughs. Grunting with pain, I managed to fix a saddle and bridle onto her, opened the stable door, and led her out into the night.

We made a fine pair, one ruin riding another, but she bore my weight without protest for many miles, across the rolling Perugian landscape. I had half a loaf of rye bread in my pocket, and a little flask of water, and these sustained me until we reached the next village.

The details of my long, wearisome journey into the West need not concern these pages. I lived to find my son, to know whether he had escaped our pursuers, but encountered no word or sign of him.

I fell in with groups of travellers, merchants and pilgrims and the like, and passed through Frankia and Gaul, living off the charity of strangers. My damaged state, and claim to be a holy man travelling back from visiting Our

Lord's sepulchre in Jerusalem, melted the hearts of many.

Only once during my wanderings, in the far west of Amorica, did I pick up a faint trace of my son. I found an abbey, a small place perched on a bluff overlooking gentle seas, where the brethren were kind and offered me shelter.

The abbey was dedicated to Saint Armel, a local soldier-saint whose jawbone rested inside a jewelled casket on the altar.

"Armel is a recent saint," explained the abbot, "when I was a boy, he came to Amorica from Britain, gravely wounded and accompanied by a few of his warriors. He was a great soldier in his time, the Bear of Britain."

My heart thumped as I gazed upon the casket. I heard my mother's voice, drifting across the long years, telling me how my grandsire's body was never found after the final slaughter at Camlann.

"Arthur vanished into the mists," Eliffer's soft voice echoed in the vaults of memory, "borne away, some say, across the sea to the Isle of Avalon. He waits there, immortal, until Britain shall have need of him again."

Armel is an Amorican variant on Arthur, but sufficiently different for my grandsire to shelter under it. Here, in this quiet house of God, he recovered from his wounds and spent his old age in prayer, far away from the endless treachery of men.

The uncertainty of Arthur's demise gave rise to the legend of his return: a sleeping warlord, waiting under a cave in the mountains of Avalon, surrounded by his warriors. One day, the horn shall blow, and summon them all to their duty.

I could hardly speak as I looked upon the mortal remains of my grandsire. Taking my silence for awed reverence, the abbot continued his story.

"Some three months ago, a young man came to this abbey. He pretended to be a pilgrim, but I could tell he was a fighting man. The soldier shone through, even under his soiled and ragged garb."

"He seemed to know all about our saint. I left him alone here to pray awhile. Then he left. He said little, and never gave his name."

The abbot was taken by surprise as I started to weep, and kindly helped me kneel before the altar. I knew the identity of his mysterious visitor.

Arthur had come here to worship the remains of his ancestor. It seemed strangely fitting that they should come together in such a fashion. God had granted me the knowledge of their meeting.

I might have made my home there. The brethren would have welcomed me, a sinful man come to spend his last days in fasting and prayer. But I still cherished the hope of one day finding my son, and feeling his warm embrace again.

It was sheer vanity. I had been given all the mercy I deserved, and could not hope for more. I left the abbey, and wandered a little while longer, until God guided my faltering steps to the Abbey of Rhuys in the south of Amorica.

And Gildas. He took me in, the great churchman and scholar of our age, even though I was of the line of Arthur, whose memory he despised.

Here I have remained, inside these blessed walls, for the best part of twenty years. I have little hope of seeing my son again, but all my prayers go to him. Let him find peace, O Lord, and trust not in the words of princes.

As for Caledfwlch, I trust Arthur has long since thrown it into the sea. Let the Flame of the West be doused forever. Caesar's sword was nothing but a bane, sent by the Devil to drag all the men of my blood to ruin.

Where are the horsemen now, where the heroes gone?
Where is the jewelled city, and where the towers
of silver and gold? Where are all the joys of battle?
Alas for the dimmed eye, the withered frame,
The brief glory of the warrior. That time is

over,
Passed into night as it had never been
Into shadow.

   Into shadow. The long night beckons for me, and I lay down my pen.

END

AUTHOR'S NOTE

The final part of the *Caesar's Sword* trilogy takes place during the end of Belisarius' first campaign in Italy (537-40) and the start of the campaign led by Narses (551-554). Despite his physical weaknesses and lack of military experience, Narses proved to be a superb general, and eventually drove the Goths out of Italy. When the Franks tried to invade the country, he smashed them too, and spent his last years repairing and reorganising the war-torn Roman homeland.

Narses succeeded where Belisarius failed, largely because the Emperor Justinian gave his favourite all the support he had denied his general. Justinian's reasons for distrusting Belisarius are unclear. He may not have been 'the last great general of Rome', as Lord Mahon called him, but Belisarius was unfailingly loyal and did everything his Emperor asked of him. Perhaps Justinian was all too aware of the fate of previous emperors at the hands of ambitious generals, and was tainted by envy of Belisarius' military talents.

Thankfully, the career of Belisarius did not end with his ignominious recall from the second Italian campaign. In 559 the aged Justinian summoned him from retirement to repel an invading horde of Bulgars. With just a handful of his old Veterans and a rabble of civilian militia, Belisarius won a final victory against the odds, defeating the enemy host and driving them out of Roman territory. He died in 565, probably not blinded and in disgrace, as one old story claims, but peacefully on his estate at Rufinianae.

Saint Armel was a real person, a holy man or 'soldier-saint' living in Brittany in the early to mid-6th century. Various writers have identified him with the historical Arthur, claiming that the tale of Arthur's journey to the Isle of Avalon after Camlann was inspired by his retreat into exile in Brittany. However dubious historically, the story has a certain charm, so I chose to make use of it.

As for the location of Caledfwlch – known to later generations as Excalibur – and the destiny of the second Arthur, Coel's son, these remain a mystery…

Made in the USA
Middletown, DE
27 August 2015